A MAN WITHOUT TALENT

BOOK ONE

DAVID COTTER

Copyright © 2024 David Cotter

Cover art by Daniel Burgess

The content contained within this book may not be reproduced, duplicated, or transmitted without direct written permission from the author or the publisher.

Under no circumstances will any blame or legal responsibility be held against the publisher, or author, for any damages, reparation, or monetary loss due to the information contained within this book, either directly or indirectly.

Legal Notice:

This book is copyright protected. It is only for personal use. You cannot amend, distribute, sell, use, quote, or paraphrase any part, or the content within this book, without the author or publisher's permission.

Disclaimer Notice:

Please note that the information contained within this document is for educational and entertainment purposes only. All effort has been executed to present accurate, up-to-date, reliable, complete information. No warranties of any kind are declared or implied. Readers acknowledge that the author is not rendering legal, financial, medical, or professional advice. The content within this book has been derived from various sources. Please consult a licensed professional before attempting any techniques outlined in this book.

By reading this document, the reader agrees that under no circumstances is the author responsible for any losses, direct or indirect, that are incurred due to the use of the information in this document, including, but not limited to, errors, omissions, or inaccuracies.

乞丐怀珠

枉受贫穷

CONTENTS

☰

Meditation (June 20, 2023)   9

—

The Trembling of the Veil	23
Dublin	37
Temples	57
A Bidniz Man	75
Aihua / 爱华	89
The Beijing Underground	121
Aihua Classic	135
The Leftward Path	155
Brief Flowering	189
10,000 Years of History	201

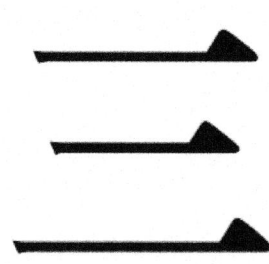

MEDITATION (JUNE 20, 2023)

Hovering at the nostrils. Reduced to a meniscus of perception. Slowly in, slowly out, wave's edge sliding forward, sinking back. Always the one sea.

That memory still so vivid, like a cartoon. I was three or four, at the beach. Must have been Port Noo or Port Rush. We were living in Belfast so probably Port Rush. They said let's go to the beach. Ranks of white cloud in blue sky, the white edge of the waves, an eternity of sand. Gone now: still here with me.

Mustn't watch the white edges furling and unfurling. Mustn't see anything. Must be empty and still. A mirror.

I AM
just sitting
fishing quiet
for samadhi.

The children sidelong this ghostly thing. Shuffling under a shroud of pain, long straggling hair hanging down. No hellooo! *Lao wai!*

The way is a long single track. Avoid veering off on devious routes. Mind becomes cluttered with structures of habit. Dismantle these. Mountains of words making meaningless selves: dismantle, diminish.

World politics. Pelosi needed to visit Taiwan, of course. Westerners don't know how much these things mean to the Chinese. They glance at me darkly. Old outsider.

Delusions. Swipe left. Be quiet.

Seven Armies ransacked the Summer Palace: now sanctions and exclusion. Bullying.

What we? Who am I? What must they see? They must hate me. My bossy ostrich beak. My empty blue eyes. Even Lin Zhi? Chen Xi? No. They love me.

I know Hulaoshi is wrong. Milefo was the first Buddha in Fahaisi. I remember. He laughed down at me when I lifted my head up out of the toilet in that club in Sanlitun. In *The*

Sutra of Perfect Enlightenment he asks: if we need to break all attachments to find enlightenment, how can we love a wife, child, friends? How? With love that is compassion, Lin told me. I must read this again. I could never cut these ties. Not for anything. I would bear a hundred hells.

I almost gave up on *The Sutra of Perfect Enlightenment* at Everything is Filth; I thought no, no more life loathing, but then I hit that awesome *however,* when the Buddha mind is awakened, and fear and desire are wiped away, then everything is holy and pure, and I could feel this was true, had known it for years. Click does the trick. Perspective.

Are these pictures or words? Must be pictures—otherwise it wouldn't be so hard to put into words. Not just pictures either, not only. Not a series of stills, a stream of consciousness at 24 frames per second. Inchoate feelings—fears, desires, glom onto everything.

Sweep away Sky Flowers; an earworm. Like food, a passing fancy Davey reminded me. Draw them back, draw back from them: quiet, emptiness.

What will you do when you wake up, she asked?

The morning we left Ireland I dreamed I was a Christmas tree. The bird songs through the open window were lights flickering in my body.

In, up. Out, down. Slowly. Again.

June 20, 2023, Dublin airport. Business class. Transfer in Stockholm. Some Chinese guys put a small pile of luggage in the Business class line. We are Bidniz class, said an impatient Chinese lady dragging her bags between the cordons. I helped a disabled white guy in a wheelchair board. I had to move their bags out of the way to get his chair through. I held his flesh, helped hoist him. He could not speak, but grunted gratefully.

Heard them say in Chinese what is the trembling old foreigner travelling to China for? They could have meant me. I told them in Chinese he is sick, travelling to China for Chinese medicine. The Business class *gemers* grunted and looked away– couldn't believe I was Business class and could speak Chinese. Didn't like it.

The Champagne didn't flow as freely as I'd have liked. I was like some debauched old Ozzy Osbourne of the TEFL world– no suit, no tie, only sadness and memories.

I swung myself stiff-legged down the aisles to check on Lin and Davey back in Economy. Squeezed in there they did not begrudge me. I couldn't have done this– my knees and hips would seize, my ass would grind and sear.

I hadn't had a drink in months, but took tomato juice and vodka as I always do on a flight. The imprint of me.

I dreaded coming here with my new body, and all its grinding pain. I had made some progress towards achieving the beginnings of stillness, but it was inevitable that Lin's preparations for our journey would require me to engage karma again, and I was afraid.

Beijing Airport. Russian script on Covid-checking machines. Angry faces in uniform. Glorious military. Power. Dragging bags. Lin and Davey don't let me carry any. All my slipped discs.

We part at Customs– they go to the intake for Chinese Nationals and I to the one for foreign nationals. Angry and officious officers. No photo here! Show me your phone one said to the Pakistani guy behind me. Barking orders in bad English. Show me your invitation. Grand inquisitors. Huddled poor. Lady in rainbow sari with four little kids. I smile at them; they turn away. Little birds. Lin and Davey are on the other side. *Wo de airen, wo de erzi.* They check with her I'm not lying.

Taxis refusing to take us. Because I am white? Long drive. Despair. Here again. The Fifth Ring Road westward. Shimmering heat and rancour. Beep beep. Beep fucking beep.

Pullmans, in Shijingshan. This run down room. The cartoon policeman aiming his gun at you. Stinking carpet I kneel on now. Check in with Trusted House Sitters. Big Ares. Rose trellis in full bloom. The house was looking so good when we left. Lin did so much to prepare. The new tarmac and paving. The gates. Stirring up karma.

Wipe it away. Come back to now, hover at the nostrils. The One me that ever was. In and Up. Out and Down. A lazy butterfly sunning itself.

41 degrees; swing along on the good leg. The sky glaring down on us, the heat rushing up at us savagely. My condition. *La mian* pulled by a smiling *gemer* with muslim cap. Pulling them out, slapping them down. Old Beijing. Happy sweating over those noodles in the grungy noodle *guar*. Davey saying how the ground seems to lift and fall in China, like a slow motion trampoline. Tell him how I felt this too during my first day in China. We talk about cicadas.

Keep seeing kids I think were my students. Have to remind myself they would all be adults now.

No social media. No BBC or Guardian. Soft power, but how will I sleep? Insomnia; jet legs. Only Tik Tok. Stick insects girls with blank masks. China Daily worse than useless. Angry and belligerent jingoism. Evening news analysis of China's military superiorities in Taiwan and South China Sea followed by documentaries about the soldiers who will drive the amphibious tanks when the time comes. On Tik Tok criminals in shackles shuffle along wearing placards naming their crimes, guided by police to where they are shot in the back of the head. Old footage of Japanese soldiers torturing Chinese people, the pornography of Nationalism. Putin's face floating among pink hearts.

Electric cars and mandatory seatbelts. No more money; all payment made through WeChat. Faces in phones. Dystopia Now. Surveillance State. Delivery men whizzing past from every direction. No more *dapaidans*; no dancing grannies.

Delusions. Swipe left.

Lin's parents putting food on our plates, not eating anything themselves. You knew the bits they asked you to eat were the bits they thought looked tastiest, that they were concerned we got enough. I said this custom seemed strange to us who had enough, getting Lin's hackles up. She said you have never been poor.

Her mom told us how when she was pregnant with Lin they chased her to try to make her abort. Fourth child. *Si mao*. Someone hid her away in a root cellar. Chuckling while she told the story as though it was the grandest lark. She is beautiful despite all the wrinkles. Every face is beautiful. Now I can feel that. She massaged my aching knee. Her ancient hands.

Blind masseuse clearing channels. Once I would have felt repulsed by his touch. Lin asked, worried, is this ok with you, but I felt love for his floppy touch.

Davey catches me sneaking back from a cig. Why do I smell smoke? Our secret. Prepare Chinese medicine. Four kinds of horses; four kinds of men. Earworm. You think you're something different but you do it all again. Trembling now. Don't let Davey see. So many tears.

Shake the earworms out. Come back to now. In, up and over, out, down and under. Slow it down.

Think I see visions but they are floaters. All delusions. Swipe left. Be empty again.

Tonight sneak a beer, write out stream of consciousness all that's crashing in on me. Open eyes a moment. Davey there playing iPad. We hover 17 stories above Babaoshan, resting place of the Glorious Communist Dead. When I lived here near the subway station 21 years ago and told people I lived at Babaoshan they laughed. Was never allowed to visit Eight Treasure Mountain. Now can't even visit Badachu. Siddhartha's tooth. Army there. No foreigner come here! No! Foreigner not allowed!

What should we do with these lives we find ourselves living? See Wisdom and Compassion as one: this is the Way. First feel compassion for yourself, then recognise we are all one, all these drifting, floating sparks of consciousness. Give up on understanding. These are only words.

Close my eyes. Wake up.

Lin with parents at Tian an men. We will leave for the mountain village when they get back. With Cherry Doudou and her husband, Li Yue and her kids. More temples. Incense. Singing bowls. I will pray to the pearl sewn in my cloak. Big Mind together. If we are only quiet enough. So hard to be quiet inside. Lin says the imprint of me is so big.

Should pack. Meditation difficult with Davey's running commentary on Plants vs Zombies, but after all these years....

Little trembling weepings can't stop them. With Chen Fu yesterday. The last last goodbye I think. How much I loved him. Not in my head, in my heart. I didn't even know. Little gaspings again.

Brother, why are you poor? It was there all along.

Cleaning Lady helped me open the Chinese medicine. Big smile and bad teeth. Kind and lovely Chinese character. From the poor and simple. Scorpions and beetles ground down. Get it down in gulps. Faith. This will ease your pain, get you on your feet again.

When I can't sleep tonight I will write this. Make what wasn't words seem words. The Dao that can be told is not the eternal Dao. The name that can be named is not the eternal name. The nameless is the beginning of heaven and earth. The named is the mother of ten thousand things.

The untying of knots that leads to 25 Bodhisattva enlightenments in the *Surangama Sutra*. You don't untie a knot by pulling one end or the other, but by pulling the knot from within: the knot of seeing and what is seen, of hearing and what is heard; cancel pain by travelling into it, asking who feels what is felt. Dismantle words too from within words, slacken this choking knot. Surrender then: there is nothing to untie.

Lunch with Liu Hao yesterday at The Big Pear. His mom and dad both dead. I see the little boy beneath the big tattoos. Trembly tears take me. I slip out for a cig. Davey follows to make sure I'm not smoking. Sees the tears, understands, hugs me. What can we do for Liu Hao, this little boy who has become so big. Whoever said that life was fair my mom used to say. Holding me off. My clumsy stupid Chinese. *Ai ni*, I blubber. The little boy's scared eyes, delicate lashes. Push his hands away and hug him tight, tighter still. He says *shi, hao jiou mei zhen ni*. Fight not to cry with all watching.

All of time is one moment. All at once happening all at once.

Lin will go to her hometown, visit her sister's grave. Davey and I will go to Hainan to see Chen Xi. Love and no remorse.

The stupid little trembles again, Davey here what does he think of his weepy dad. Crying everywhere, any trigger, can't stop. Melting into water, shivery water.

Flood of consciousness. All moments are as one at once. Big mind. The imprint of me. How to erase it? Have tried so hard, in so many ways. You have to cut the fourth horse to the very bone. Not one thought after another. That's not how it works. Not a stream, but a flood. Flooding in. Always forever.

Milefo was there at the first stage. The Buddha to come. First in any temple. At the top temple three more golden Buddhas. Amitofo Center. Pure Land. We pray. Dashizhi and Wisdom to the left. Guanyin and Compassion to the right.

We kowtow and pray, all of us. I weep, of course. Breath in, Wisdom, breath out and down Compassion. Wisdom. Compassion. Wisdom. Compassion. In and up, out and down.

This Great Ocean, here at my feet, churning up all moments I have lived.

THE TREMBLING OF THE VEIL

I first travelled to Beijing in the summer of 2000, when I was thirty five years old. I flew with Chen Xi from Dublin through Helsinki to Beijing to be married. When we arrived in Beijing, some of our baggage had been lost in the transfer. Chen Xi had an uncle who worked at the airport, and he came down with big smiles and clasped hands, to help us arrange for the bags to be delivered when they were found. He led us out of the baggage claim area into Arrivals, to where Chen Xi's parents and some members of her family were waiting at a wall beside sliding glass doors. There were raucous greetings in Chinese and I was ushered into the back of another uncle's black Audi. Chen Xi called this uncle Seven Uncles, although I always thought his name should have been Seventh Uncle, because he was the seventh and youngest brother of Chen Xi's father. He had spent time in prison as a young man, over a game to see who dared to stab himself deepest in the thigh. The people in the car addressed me directly in Chinese and I leered my ostrich beak back at them. They kept saying *Beijing tebie da*. Sometimes Chen Xi translated and I replied, yup, it is, or wow, which she translated back to them. I was disorientated, and my reaction was to invoke in myself a spirit of hilarity.

Visiting China had never been one of my dreams. I just found myself there. So many buildings, so much cement; so overwhelmingly man-made. We drove from the airport along Beijing's 5th ring road to Shijingshan, in the extreme west of Beijing, at the edge of the mountains. Chen Xi pointed out the pagodas of Badachu, its eight holy places, nestled among the forested slopes. She told me that the highest of these eight holy places held Siddhartha's tooth. The people in the car stroked my forearms and said sweetly *mao mao hou*: hairy monkey. I had to push Chen Xi for translation on this, and when I understood everyone laughed and I mimicked a monkey. They taught me how to mimic a monkey in Chinese, with one hand curled back over the brow like a salute in reverse.

We exited the 5th Ring Road to the right, onto Chang An Jie at Bajiou Youleyuan, the amusement park, with its dusty, Disneyland castle. Shijinghan District was to be my home for the 16 years that I would spend in China. Shijingshan means 'stone scenic mountain,' but it is said that this derives from 'wet holy-manuscript mountain.' When Tang San Zhang returned from India with Siddhartha's manuscript, he dropped it in Yong Ding River when the turtle that was carrying him and his disciples across the river submerged itself. Tan Sang Zhang climbed a hill and spread the manuscript out on a stone, where it dried in the sun. Tang San Zhang's journey to retrieve Siddhartha's manuscript is told in *Journey to the West*. There were endless interpretations of *Journey to the West* on Chinese TV, and sometimes I would watch these with Chen Xi and her family.

There was a little Thomas the Train ride for babies outside a local shop, and it played a beautiful song about the *Journey to the West*. I learned to sing this in Chinese.

White Dragon Horse
hooves toward the west
carries Tang San Zhang
and three disciples follow.

What evil spirits, ghosts, monsters, devils?
What succubi in gaudy makeup?
What difficult paths through mountains of knives, traps and fire?

At the end of Chang An Jie, where it stops at the entry to Shougang Iron and Steel, we turned northwest and followed the edge of the steel mill for about five kilometres to reach Chen Xi's family home. The steel mill appeared to me a vast, steam-punk dystopia of pipes and furnaces: a post-apocalyptic fun park. It was filled with rusty cathedrals of iron, and there were two enormous chimneys. In the centre, a three-tiered pagoda stood on a lone hill in silhouette.

Chen Xi's parents lived on the top floor of an apartment block of four stories, among a maze of identical four story buildings in Moshikou, just north of the Shougang Iron and Steel Mill. The stairwell was of bare, grimy concrete. There was no graffiti, but there were business cards pasted to the walls, and patches of glue and paper where they had been scraped away. There were tidy piles of Chinese cabbages in front of some doors. On the heavy, iron door of their home were gleaming red posters of an ornate Chinese character, *shuang xi*. This character means double happiness, and it had been placed there to recognise our marriage. Over the coming days I saw this character again and again. The apartment was small and chaotic, full of relatives laughing, chatting and snacking on things I'd never imagined. The smells were powerful, and they were different to anything I'd encountered, hints of other secret worlds. I remember windows open and light and breeze flooding into the apartment. I remember sweating the whole time I was there. I felt alien, even to myself, and this sensation of apartness filled me with excitement. With everyone speaking in Chinese, I was left alone with my thoughts, feeling like a sort of ghost.

Chen Xi and I went for a walk with her mother. The heat was insistent and the blue sky pressed down on us. We weaved through an open market. The fierce sun had reduced the earth to a fine powder shrouding the road. Whenever a motorbike passed, a cloud of yellow dust lifted into the air. Trays of food, clothing, and knick-knacks were attended by people fanning themselves and staying out of the sun. Men pulled their shirts up over their bellies with nonchalance. They nursed and coddled these bellies. Everyone stared at me as I passed. I was dizzy from the heat, and the sensory overload of the market, seething with people, odour and noise. We went up a winding hill between tea houses, little restaurants and traditional medicine clinics. It was quieter here. Rows of grannies in pink satin were practising Tai Chi among the trees. Old people were tending to their bodies: rubbing, patting, swinging little maces with nubbed plastic balls over their shoulders onto their backs. Crackly transistor radios in bicycle baskets played traditional Chinese music. There was a man with crickets in grass cages, and they taught me to say *gergu*, everyone crowding round and laughing. An old couple lounged in the shade among bee hives selling honey. Higher up the winding path toward the temple, there were ramshackle shops selling incense and Buddhist trinkets. Chen Xi bought a big bundle of pink incense and she and her mother chattered in Chinese. An urgent, metallic whirring had been following me. I peered into the trees, seeking its source.

When Chen Xi found 'cicada' in her electronic dictionary, and told me that they were whirring their wings to cool down, I recalled my father stooping to show my brother Deane and me a dead cicada. We were in Heritage Park, Calgary, Alberta. He told us that on his first day in Africa he'd heard the whirring of cicadas, and couldn't figure out what it was. My father grew up in Northern Ireland, and in 1960, after finishing his degree in geology at Queen's University, he took a job in Tanganyika, at Williamson's Diamond Mine. I wondered if that day, as he puzzled at the sound of cicadas, beneath a blue sky pressing down heat and mirage, among an alien people, he felt the world open up for him as I felt the world opening up for me now, walking up to the the gates of Fahai Si.

There was no grass, only yellow clay, packed down by the passage of countless feet. I saw a bit of stone broken from the shell of a turtle statue, pressed into the dry earth at an angle, functioning as a stepping stone. Chen Xi told me that things like this had been broken and scattered during the Cultural Revolution. At the top of the hill we reached the gates of Fahai Si, a temple built at the time of Shakespeare.

The temple was quiet and we paused in each of the open courtyards in our ascent toward the highest point. The corners of roofs curled upward, and little figures perched on these. Chen Xi told me that they were there so demons could not sit on the corners of the roofs. She explained that the Feng Shui here was powerful, and though I felt obliged to scoff at this, it seemed that we had stepped outside of time; that I was being lifted gently, and gently dropped, with the pulse of the world. Fahai Si is famous for its frescoes of blue gods and elephant-headed demons. In the cool shadows of the fabulous dark between courtyards, these images seemed more Hindu than Buddhist; the tusked blue gods with perfect toes and horned demons boiling lost souls in cauldrons. We moved up through the stations of the temple and Chen Xi explained that the walks up the stairs between levels of the temple represented the struggles of the soul in its ascent toward enlightenment.

People burned bundles of long, pink incense sticks in front of a fat, golden Buddha on a dais at the top of a flight of stairs. He had enormous earlobes, like Chen Xi and her mother. The trails of smoke drifted dreamily, and unravelled in the still air. I felt that this Buddha was laughing at me, trying to catch my eye; about to let me in on a secret.

Bald monks in saffron gowns passed like spirits from room to room. One was sweeping with slow strokes in the shade. We stood beneath two ancient trees, looking up at people holding sticks of incense to their brows, bowing three times before the jolly, golden Buddha, then standing the incense sticks upright in an ornate brazier that was full to the rim with ash. The ancient trees, most of their bark stripped away to the smooth, silver flesh beneath, reminded me of the smooth, red flesh of the arbutus trees in front of my father's cabin on Lasqueti Island. I stood watching the incense drift between the laughing Buddha and me. This was one of those times when the world around me seemed to shimmer. My eyes blurred, head rushed and I saw patches of black, as though something was moving just behind the visible world. I wish there was a way to say this, to hold onto all of these moments surging into nothingness, to paint a picture of a time and place with words and so save all of us from dying, but I have always failed.

We left the temple's odour of sanctity, walked back down through the market and past Chen Xi's family home to *Da Yar Li*: the Big Pear. At either side of the steps leading up to the restaurant was a stone lion with one paw holding down a ball. On entering I saw again the same fat, laughing Buddha as in the temple, in an alcove on a table with fruit, incense and a bowl of rice in front of him. I remarked to Chen Xi that this was not a typical Buddha, serene and with eyes closed, and she told me that this was Mi Le Fu. She said most people think he is a God of wealth, but they don't understand. She typed into her electronic dictionary, and showed me the word *compassion*.

We were led by waitresses in traditional blue and white *chipa* into a big room at the back of the restaurant where there were three round tables and about twenty of Chen Xi's extended family milling about, not sitting. Chen Xi held my arm and told me to wait and see where I was asked to sit. Seven Uncles sat at the top of the central table, facing the door, and I was called to sit beside him. There was shuffling, voices and commotion as they worked out where everyone else would sit. Everyone was seated, and there were three or four waitresses in attendance. Dish after dish was placed on the lazy Susan, and spun around in front of me, where Seven Uncles placed a choice morsel from each onto the dish beside my rice bowl. They were all amazed that I could use chopsticks. I showed them that I could lift three peanuts at once with my chopsticks, and everyone had a go. The food was strange, varied and exquisite.

I was surprised to discover how much Chinese people like to drink. We drank a mild Beijing lager, *Yanjing*, but they also opened bottles of *baijiu*, a powerful spirit made from rice. We drank this from small glasses. There were repeated calls to *ganbei*, which Chen Xi translated as bottoms up, though it literally means dry glass. The *baijiu* was revolting; it tasted like poison. During my first years I tried to discover something that could be mixed with *baijiu*, to make it more palatable, but there was nothing that could cover its morbid spices. Among waving cat ornaments there were huge, glass vats of *baijiu*, with snakes and scorpions floating in them. I was expected to finish off the glass each time someone raised a glass to me and called out *ganbei*. Chen Xi urged me to drink strategically, to avoid drinking one on one, and to instead involve as many other people as I could in each *ganbei*. This was sound advice, but it took me years to accept this wisdom. I found that downing a class of *baijiu* was most manageable when followed by a swig of beer. Courteous words of welcome preceded calls to *ganbei*, and Chen Xi translated these for me, then translated back my replies of gratitude. We stood and held eye contact as we knocked back the *baijiu*. They had beautiful, smiling eyes, delicate lashes. When we clinked glasses, they tried to clink lower on the rim of my glass, and when Chen Xi explained this was a way of showing respect, I tried to clink lower on their glasses. This became a game, with us lowering our glasses below the level of the table, seeking to clink lower on the rim of the other's glass. We were all happy and laughing.

The men were heavy smokers, and whenever someone went for a cigarette they handed me one, and lit it for me. When I lit a cigarette for someone they tapped the back of my hand with two fingers as thank you. When I filled someone's glass of *baijiu* they rapped two knuckles on the table. Seven Uncles had a long pinky nail, which indicated that he didn't need to do physical labour. I considered how inconvenient this pinky nail must have been. He often itched his face with it. He had a sloping forehead and his hair was slicked back. He had the look of a snake. A leather man-purse sat beside his dishes. When on the move he carried it tucked under his arm. No man I knew back home would have carried such a bag, for fear of being mocked. I realised that the stereotypes and foibles that had such influence on me were irrelevant here in China. I could make myself anew here, in any way that I saw fit. They tried to get me to smoke expensive brands of cigarettes, but I soon found the brand that suited me, and I stuck with the humble *lingdiarbade* Zhong Nan Hai throughout my time in China. My first proficiency in Chinese was to be able to ask for these in a shop. Eventually, I got to the point where I would just go in and say *diar ba*, point eight, but that was a long way off from my first afternoon in Beijing.

When we came out of the Big Pear, I was surprised to find

that it was still day-time. I was quite drunk, and I teetered up under the blue sky, savouring vertigo. I felt I had been torn from my world, and inserted into this alternate reality. I might as well have been on Mars. We walked toward the shaggy hills behind the low-rise apartment blocks. There was a heat haze, and water mirages nestled in the sagging tarmac. People huddled in shade, fanning themselves. T-shirts were up over bellies and trouser legs were rolled up to the knee, more often than not on only one leg. There were little barber shops, massage parlours, make-shift restaurants and internet cafes. The language seemed so abrasive, and there were savage Chinese characters on billboards everywhere. There was a dusty Santa Claus in the window of a little restaurant. People watched me as I passed, and pointed me out to one another. Occasionally someone called out Hal-loooo. I smiled and grinned at everyone. The people were modest, happy and gentle. There were many beautiful women, but the fashion sense was purposely naive, with flip flops, tights, hello kitty t-shirts, even jammies. Some couples wore matching outfits. The women tried to keep out of the sun under floppy sun bonnets and parasols, because dark skin meant you worked in the fields. I pointed out to Chen Xi that in the west, people wanted a tan because dark skin meant you had leisure time to spend out in the sun, whereas pale skin meant you had to work in an office. An old woman took one look at me and her twinkling face began to cackle. A young guy followed me down the road, shouting Billie Corrigan! Billie Corrigan! I love Billie Corrigan!

When we got back to Chen Xi's family home, we were alone with her parents and her brother, Chen Wei. We sat on the sofa watching *Journey to the West* on TV. The decor in the sitting room was sombre and dark, with red wood panels on the walls, making the room seem smaller. I drank more *Yanjing* beer. We snacked on seeds. Chen Xi's mom was pudgy, cute, and always smiling. She had been studying English in anticipation of my arrival. She said to me, how are you, again and again, like a little song. She had an ornate and formal posture to accompany the question. Chen Xi's father was thin, dignified, and full of scorn. On his forehead was an indelible grey smear that seemed to be of ash or dust. His attitude was no-nonsense: he looked down on most things, and approved of very little. Chen Xi's mother and father had been sent to the countryside during the Cultural Revolution, and Chen Xi had been raised by her grandmother. I presumed that there were many things that were never spoken of, secrets and stories. Chen Xi had the look of her mother but the character of her father. She and her father had dreadful arguments. Whenever they spoke, in fact, it seemed that they were arguing.

Chen Wei slept on the windowed balcony with its potted palms. Chen Xi took me into the room in which she had grown up. This was to be our room during our stay. She pointed out that her parents had put air-conditioning in the house because they weren't sure that I would be able to bear the heat, but she didn't want us to use it because it made the air dry and unhealthy. The room had dolls and children's toys in it. The wardrobes were overflowing. Chen Wei's computer was running a stock market program. The bed was covered in a sheet of bamboo tiles, which allowed rivulets of sweat to run from the body. We slept with no sheets or blankets. This was the first time I had ever done so. We lay on the tiles in our underpants. I tried to pull Chen Xi to me, but she whispered that she couldn't, here with her parents so close. Before we slept I heard Chen Xi's father hacking up phlegm in the toilet beside our room.

This was her room, her world. She looked at me and laughed kindly.

DUBLIN

I first met Chen Xi when I was a library assistant at Griffith College, Dublin. She'd left China to do a Hospitality Management course in Switzerland, and then come to Dublin as a transfer student for a final year of Business Studies, after which she planned to do six months of work placement. I first saw her from the window of the security hut where I spent my nights with Sable, the Alsatian.

I completed my doctorate at Trinity College, in 1996. I wrote about the sexual perversity I saw at the heart of Joyce's work. I was content down in the Lecky library with a stack of old, obscure books beside me, and I felt that to do doctorate after doctorate would have been the perfect life.

During my time in Dublin I made many enemies. I shared a flat overlooking Merrion Square with Alex Frazer, who set up the TV-commercial department of Assets Model Agency on Baggot Street. He was famous locally for having been a prominent extra in *The Cook, the Thief, the Wife and her Lover*. I used to follow him around the bars and nightclubs, watching how, no matter how crudely and disrespectfully he and his cronies spoke to women, these women would throw themselves at him. The women they targeted would at first be shocked by their rudeness, and they would begin to counter attack, and this would develop into sexual frisson. He was humorous and irreverent, and I hated him. He told everyone that I had punched him in the face with keys between my knuckles, but that is not what I intended. He was trying to raise my rent on our apartment in Merrion Square, and when I gave him the rent minus the arbitrary hike, he followed me up the sidewalk from the ATM along Merrion Square, badgering me. I turned around and kicked him in the thigh; he grabbed my leg. When I pushed back against his face I just happened to have my keys in hand. The police came and got me out of the apartment, took away my weapons, including a Ghurka knife I'd inherited when my grandmother died, and my little nodge of hash. I moved to Stoney Batter for a while, before sliding lower, to Seville place, off Sherif Street, just round the corner from the Five Lamps. Going in and out I never looked anyone in the eye. Winter was dark. There were many other incidents which shone an unfavourable light on my character, and made me unpopular on Grafton Street. I kept a sharpened pencil in my hand. These incidents were all related to my desperation concerning women, and exacerbated by my belief that I was a tough guy. I won some boxing matches as a middle-weight but then I was humiliated in a tournament against UCD in the Trinity Exam Hall in front of Valerie Ringrose Fitzsimons and a roaring, laughing crowd, when I discovered that I have a glass jaw.

I talked to a PhD student from Syria in the Buttery Bar at Trinity. We talked about my thesis, and when I spoke about self flagellation and self renunciation he was all with me: very interesting, it is like my religion. When I went on to tell him this self abasement was performed before the feminine principle as audience, as an act of atonement for what the sublimated masculine urges would have subjected her to, he threw the table over me and stood up. He was a tough looking guy, and he had been in the army. His eyes were blazing, and I made a show of standing up to him, but made sure we didn't actually engage.

I defended my PhD dissertation to Terence Brown and Declan Kiberd. Terence asked how I could base a point upon the claim that the masturbatory experience is riotous, and driven by its own compulsion to profusion. I replied that this was my experience. Terence conceded that he could not comment on this. Declan giggled in his chair like a leprechaun. He was enthusiastic about my dissertation, my take on the new, womanly man, and he urged me to get it published. After I finished my doctorate though, I was lost. I had no idea of how to proceed, and how to begin to make my own living. I was dependent on my father's money, and I spent a lot.

When I knew I had the doctorate, I left Dublin and went to stay with my cousins at Dergmoney, their country home in Omagh. The house was over a hundred years old, and surrounded by fields which were sold off one by one to the encroaching housing estates. When we were kids, I would take out a grey pony, Thunderbolt, and Warnock would ride out on his own red pony, Breakaway Boy. When I was at Trinity the house had become a hippy Mecca. One morning I rode Judge McMiniman's Rockfield Badger, and Warnock the Red Admiral, through the last of the fields, under canopies of oak trees. The ground was hard and frosty, and there were plumes of breath above us.

The hippy idyll, though, was doomed by economics—I was hanging around in a second floor room trying to write. There was no heating and we were all freezing. None of us had any money, and we would find and pilfer one another's hoardings. One day Warnock was down in the yard, taking care of the horses, and he started to speak to me in a funny voice, as though he were addressing a gentleman. I let it get to me.

A little later we were all on mushrooms in the ancient kitchen, and I bear hugged Warnock, pressing into his collarbone with my chin, and pulling his lower spine towards mine with clasped hands. Warnock asked one of his friends, Paul Doc, to help him sort me out, and it was clear that I had overstayed my welcome at Dergmoney House.

I got my dad to buy me a ticket back to Calgary. I spotted my father and his new wife, Netty, at Arrivals. The cold was shocking as we shuffled over icy sidewalks to my father's mini van. Streetlights lit hoar frosted branches from within like icy chandeliers. Calgary appeared pristine at minus twenty; my mother had called it a moon-base when she was dying. She scratched at my father's throat with her red, sharpened nails; blood ran down to his white collar.

When we were very small my mother tried to fly back to Omagh with Deane and me. She had a phobia about flying, so when we got on the plane she took sleeping pills and drank vodka. Next thing I remember someone was asking if there was a doctor on the plane and then we landed somewhere in northern Canada. They took my mom off the plane in a stretcher, and they put Deane and me on another plane back to Calgary. The stewardess who looked after us was pretty. She had big hair and she told me to look after my little brother. I put my arm over his shoulder and pulled him to me. He was three years old, and I was five. At Arrivals, my dad stood with a plume of steam above his head in the night air, looking for us with his worried face from among a crowd of other faces.

Sitting behind them in the minivan, I explained my very important discovery, the topic of my PhD thesis, how all of our gestures and urges are imbued with sexual energy, and sexual energy is inherently political. Phallic sexual energy is innately sadistic, and thus appeals to the fascist-authoritarian personality. The artist and the pure soul may renounce sadism through an identification with the feminine, and the usurpation of feminine victimisation. So, it was a choice between paranoia or schizophrenia, *a la Anti-Oedipus*. The innate brutality of male sexual energy was the root of all our woes, and the sooner we all recognised this and became new, womanly men, the better. They listened quietly until we reached their new home. Netty asked me not to smoke so much.

While I had been away my father had sold our home and bought a house in a new suburb of Calgary. Entering my father's new house with my bags in hand I felt I was walking into a hall of mirrors. Stepping forward was stepping back. I resented him for not having adequately respected our dead.

Over the coming days I tried to find work, but when I spoke to someone at the University of Calgary English Department, I was told I had a snowball's chance in hell of finding academic work in Canada. Netty found me a job painting pipes in an underground parking lot. I looked out at the snow and told my father I wanted to kill myself. He said it was the Dead Can Dance cassette I kept listening to.

I was drinking a lot, hanging out with my best friend from high school, Big Al Karmis. At the end of a long, drunken evening I had somehow ruined Alex's stereo trying to play my Smashing Pumpkins cassette. Before that the scary

Greek gangster guy had made a threatening crack about having me lay my cock on the table in return for all the drinks he had been buying me that night. They had sent me back to Alex's house with a prostitute while they went to get more cocaine. Upon returning and seeing the mess I'd made of his cassette deck, Alex knocked me on my back with my head up against the door and hammered his fist into my upturned face.

My time in Calgary ended with my father diving across the bed to pull the shotgun from my mouth only a few days after he'd had an operation for prostate cancer. I kept saying it wasn't loaded as I stood looking down at him on the bed, the rifle in his grip. He tried to discharge both barrels into the wall, but there was nothing in it.

I'd put a shotgun in my mouth at Big Al's place a few days before the beating. In fact it was when I told him I would come back to his house and shoot him with my dad's shotgun that Big Al sprang at me from in front of his malfunctioning stereo and beat me to a pulp.

My dad said I couldn't come into his life like a sledgehammer. I realised there was no place for me with Netty and him in Calgary. I asked him to buy me a ticket back to Dublin. He couldn't see any other way. I was 30 years old and unable to earn a living. I dreamed of being a writer. Not so much of being a writer, as of finding a way to live to write. I had seen things, I'd had visions, I'd been witness to fissures in the fabric of reality. I knew that I was meant to be a witness, that with these fissures all around me, and festooned in ghosts, I could never become something like a businessman. To work for a company would stifle me; I would always need to be a fraud. I was embedded in a Block Universe that had begun to crumble and crack.

I moved around a few dreadful flats in Dublin. I went clubbing with Ronan McManus and the other Trinity e-fiends. I borrowed a suit from Mick Fahy and did some interviews at universities but wasn't even close to being hired. I met Eileen Gogan at Ri Ra's. She had been the singer for The Wannabees, and Morrisey had once said they were his favourite band. Within a week of lending her my copy of *Venus in Furs*, the edition with Deleuze's essay *Coldness and Cruelty*, I moved in with her. She liked my taste in music. She helped me get work as night security at Griffith College. We went to fetish clubs, Gag and Powder Bubble, and took a lot of e. She decided I was a monster, and phoned my father to tell him. I had been topping from the bottom all along, and she hated this.

Despite what Eileen might have picked up in *Venus in Furs*, my perversity was not based on feminist principles. Although I grew up in a culture where it was considered the greatest shame, I often felt it would have been easier to be gay, as then it would have been about bodies and other people, and not so tied up in an algebra of power. The problem was that my sexual arousal was founded on the desire to subjugate myself before an Ideal of feminine beauty, and be despised by the one from whom I most sought approval.

My first sexual feelings were aroused by imagining myself being ritually humiliated by my classmates, in front of the prettiest girl in the class. I could never understand why it had to be this way. I always thought the source of this compulsion was bullying at school, and the disdain on the faces of the prettiest girls when they caught me gazing at them moonily.

I created an elaborate self mythology in which the birth of the anti-self was established by a series of imaginary concessions, bringing into being a secret self indebted for its existence to these concessions to compulsion. Wherever I looked I saw a hall of mirrors. Somewhere back in the primaeval past I chose not to bring the brutality of male desire to bear on another, but to instead direct this violence against myself. Then there were two me's, one for me and one against.

Although I had been certain for so long that none of this had anything to do with my mother, I have recently become convinced that the source of my romantic malaise had more to do with her than the childhood bullying, that, in fact, the one flowed from the other.

Throughout my life the societal cyphers of dominance and meekness grew and accrued around this initial structure. I felt myself inextricably caught up in a sexually charged collision of binaries, always refuting my place in any hierarchy by turning everything upside down, turning everything into a parodic *jouissance* that made my senses tingle.

At first this was a timid whispering, a languorous dismantling of self while gazing at photos of beautiful women in my dad's Time magazines. When I found his Playboys I learned to drive myself into a frenzy looking at the photos of these women. I hated myself, and my sexuality became an expression of this hatred, and I wondered what made me this way.

Made, *made* me. I was baffled by the question of free will and compulsion. The real me did not want any of this. I renounced the fantasy a thousand times, and with tears, but the more I attempted to hold it at bay, the fiercer it grew, the deeper it would take me into the shadowplay of my humiliation and rejection.

It had always been my secret, and I imagined no one else could have suffered from such an absolute antithesis between their sexual and mundane selves. When I discovered it in Joyce, though, and other literature, the Romantics especially, I asked myself if my mode of loving was just, or merely selfishness and sloth. How could something originate in its antithesis? Truth in falsity? Strength in weakness? Or will to truth in deception? As I entered adulthood, my heart was choked with confusion.

Once this structure was established I imagined deeper and deeper humiliations upon myself, and greater distance and disdain on the part of the object of desire. When I really admired a girl, I would avoid integrating her into the fantasy at first, but once I brought her image in it became unbearably acute. I could not resist diving deeper into this rush of loss and pain. The problem was complicated, because when I was not aroused, I did not want to be humiliated. There was a terrible battle in my soul. When I saw by day the kids who had humiliated me in the shadows of my riotous desire, I hated them.

As my body grew stronger, I tried to redeem myself through violence for the humiliations I'd imagined myself suffering at their hands. I had the perhaps distorted view that women actually wanted men like the monsters that I conjured in my masturbatory imagination. Eileen may have led me on a leash to the fetish balls, but when we had sex it was missionary style; I turned my head to the side, and imagined submitting to some woman I'd seen on the street.

The stereotypical dominatrix never did it for me, or someone acting for me, playing a role. My mistress had to be distant and pure. It was a lot to ask for, I know.

Compensating for my submissive side, I hit the punching bag at Griffith College in vain attempt to vent my rage, and once when a guy had pissed in the sink at a party in the Coomb, and the hosts asked me to eject him, I grabbed him by the throat, threw him into a policeman's lock, smashed him out the kitchen doors, and whooshed him down the narrow stairs where he collapsed down the last few steps in a heap. I dragged him out onto the road by his legs. I thought that everyone would think I was a hero, but the party goers shied away from me after this.

Some weeks later Eileen called my cousins in Omagh and begged them to come down and take me away. She demanded that I leave the apartment I was sharing with her, so I found a place on Ormond Road. I left her my computer, a 286 with 4 megabytes of RAM. As I was leaving, she stroked a smoking faggot of sage along the walls of my room in an effort to expel bad energies.

The landlord at Ormond Road had an Abe Lincoln beard, and he insisted that I should keep the curtains open, even though I was on the ground floor. He felt that drawing the curtains would encourage an unhealthy lifestyle. At Griffith College, I was promoted from night security to library assistant. I joined a James Joyce mailing list and got into disputes with people who didn't like my take on Joycean sexuality. They were embarrassed by it, but I knew that I was right, and that what I had written was important. I tried to get my PhD thesis published as a book. I reworked it and sent it twice to Cambridge University Press, at Declan Kiberd's suggestion, but each time they asked for revisions. I continued going to Gag and Powder Bubble, though I was flying solo now, with no one holding the dog-lead. Politically, it wasn't great. There I was in dog collar and dangling lead, no shirt, leather trousers, slick glistening body up at the front dancing with abandon, when a big, black guy started pushing me out of his way, and giving me bad vibes. After a moment I realised that he thought I was joking about his people suffering at the hands of white guys like me. I felt so ashamed of myself. All of this unfocussed devotion was pure Sentimentality. Even if I found a girlfriend, how was I to share love with someone from whom I sought rejection and disdain? It had become so dreary. There was no hope. I kept putting myself in terrible danger.

Chen Xi hung around in the library and asked me to help her find a book. When I opened the book to answer her questions, she leaned into me. She began to stay late at the computers and when I shut down the library I would walk her home. She lived in a house in Rathmines subdivided into many tiny spaces for foreign students. She shared a toilet with a few Arab guys. The landlord was miserly with heat. After a couple of coffees, Chen Xi began to spend some nights with me on Ormond Road. She'd had her own business in Beijing, a restaurant, and she had sold it to cover the cost of studying abroad, but she didn't have much money left to support herself in Dublin. When she undressed to get into bed beside me, I noticed that she was skinny. She had to wake at four to ride her bike through the black rain to her job serving breakfast at the Davenport. The rain left red blotches on her face.

We moved together into an apartment on Rathmines Road Lower, right beside the Blackberry Market. It was one room with a single bed in one corner, and a kitchen in the other. At night, rats from the canal entered the kitchen corner and I would get up and make a racket going over to them in my underpants, hoping they would scurry away before I got any closer. The landlord gave us a lump of blue poison to put down and after a few days the rats stopped coming but the room was full of flies and the smell of death.

A group of North Africans lived downstairs from us, and sold me hash. One day they got into our apartment through the window when we were out and took everything nice. The police said we had no definitive proof that they were the ones who'd robbed us. After this we couldn't face the North Africans anymore, and we moved to a cosy flat on the top floor of 36 Beechwood Avenue, in Ranelagh.

Strolling along the tree canopied roads, Chen Xi spoke to me about marriage, and I told her that this meant nothing to me, that I had no belief in marriage. I told her how Joyce had only married Nora to look after matters of children and inheritance. She told me that if we didn't get married she would lose her visa, and she would need to return to China as soon as she finished her studies at Griffith College. A few days later I went on my own to Gag, and when I came home she was asleep. As I got undressed she woke up, and I showed her the welts and bruises I'd received that night at the fetish club. I told her that this was a part of me that I could never change. She seemed to accept what I said, though I am not certain that she understood.

I left my job at Griffith College, and started teaching EFL at Swan Training, on Grafton Street. I also got a job as a tutor to first year English students at the university in Maynooth. I met Des Fitzgibbons at Maynooth and we became buddies. He helped me get some work with the UCD Adult Education Program. Together we designed and delivered a course on reading *Ulysses*. We focussed on one chapter per week. Des became a great friend to Chen Xi and me, and our lives got better. She prepared Chinese food, and I loved this. She made Chinese dumplings, roast duck that we got vacuum packed from the Asia market, and a powerful chicken soup with strange roots and berries her mother had sent from China. We had two goldfish, and Chen Xi helped me to buy my first mobile phone. We had internet now, and I downloaded music from Napster. I put *A Whole Lotta Love* up loud and danced to it, mostly with my hips, to Chen Xi's great amusement.

Chen Xi was very nervous at the approach of the final exam for her BA in Business Studies. There would be three essay questions, and she had a good idea of what these would be. I wrote up three answers, and read them through to her, then listened to her read them back to me. When I went to bed she sat up reading these answers through again and again in a whisper. She was memorising the sound more than the meaning. This continued for a couple of weeks, until the day of the exam, when I wished her luck, and she rode her bike to Griffith College. When she got back to the apartment and I asked her how it went she sank down on the sofa and sobbed. Her eyes squeezed shut pressing tears out, and her mouth opened in an inarticulate moan. I felt protective of her, felt that it was she and I against the world. I comforted her, and told her she couldn't know yet how she had done. It turned out I was right. She received first-class honours, and the highest mark in her class.

We agreed to get married. We would go to Omagh for a legal marriage, and then travel to China that summer for the ceremony. The last time I had been to Omagh was the evening of the Omagh bomb. I was watching TV with curtains drawn at Ormond Road after a shift of night security at Griffith College. After a cowboy was shot on the roof of the saloon, and he began to roll off, a blue screen came on requesting all medical personnel make their way to Omagh. I called up to Omagh and got through to Micky Fahy, Scarlet's husband. He said he had seen the roofs all lift up off the buildings for a moment when the bomb went off. I rolled a joint and got the bus to Omagh.

That evening I drank whiskey with Warnock, Dezzy Campell and Uncle John around Scarlet's kitchen table. We set up Olympic-style wrestling matches. These guys had never wrestled at school, but my high school wrestling partner had been Owen Hart, who became a famous professional wrestler. Though he was bigger than me, and farmer-strong, I pinned Dezzy in seconds, throwing him with a great crash into the bin. I gave him a little bite on the arm, and later received a light slap on the face as rebuke for this when the tooth marks became apparent on his forearm and we all laughed. John said steady on boys, as though he was talking to horses. Scarlet came down from her sleep thinking there had been another bomb.

Chen Xi and I took the bus up to Omagh. Dergmoney had been sold and demolished, and they were all living separately in the area. It was not the same without that big house. After my mother had been diagnosed with cancer, and told she had five years to live, my parents sent me from Calgary to Dergmoney each summer when I was 13, 14 and 15. After that the people from Dergmoney visited us in Calgary, as my mother struggled through her final two years. My mother's twin sister, WIllow, lived with her husband, John, and their children, Alison (Holly), Patricia (Scarlet), and Warnock. It was a sort of Wuthering Heights. Scarlet was Cathy. Warnock and John had the darkness of Heathcliff. John was of wealthy Ulster stock, and as an only child, he'd grown up in boarding schools. His mother could not control him, and when his father died at a young age, he became master of the estate. He was a bully. My mother would sometimes complain that if John was our father we would not be so cheeky.

The world is drenched in death and pain, and almost everything we do is done to avoid recognising this. John wrecked rally cars, became involved in show jumping, and ran through his inheritance at a frantic rate. I admired Scarlet. She was wild and dangerous. She looked a bit like my mother, and I sometimes thought my mother could have been as proud, strong and brave as Scarlet if she'd only wanted to be. We travelled around the country to horse shows in a big lorry. Behind the driver's cab was a room with sofa and kitchenette, and a bed above the driver. Through a door behind this room were six big horses in partitions. I was terrified of getting the horses on and off the back of the lorry.

Some of the yard hands thought I was a great guy because I was from somewhere else. They didn't know that my parents sent me to Dergmoney so that my mother could have time away from me.

I pilfered whatever I wanted from Dergmony, believing that I was more entitled to this history than them, because they took for granted what we had lost when my father dragged us away to moon-base Calgary. I took an old book from a crowded bookcase, *The Poems of Ossian*, translated by James McPherson Esq., published 1797.

I once walked across town from Dergmoney to my grandmother's house in Gortmore Gardens. When I got there she gave me apple tart and tea. Her daughter, Rosemary, had MS, and was slumped in a wheelchair, grunting and googly-eyed. My grandmother told me that if anyone ever wanted to fight with me I should walk away, even if that person stuck a penknife in my shoulder. I went up to her attic and took a sword that had been used in the Battle of Waterloo. It was paired with a cavalry sabre that my uncle, Peter, later claimed as his own. I put the short sword in my sock, and up my trouser leg. I also stole a little bottle of booze she had in a cabinet. People were always stealing from my grandmother.

When Chen Xi and I arrived in Omagh to be married, she was shocked that my cousins offered us no food. They lived in the country so we weren't able to go and get anything. Later Chen Xi told me that she was so hungry she had stolen a banana. The next day, my cousins came with us to the relevant office for a legal wedding. The lady who married us asked if Chen Xi knew what she was doing, because Chen Xi couldn't understand her Omagh accent. It was difficult to convince her that Chen Xi could speak some English. When I repeated after the lady that I would love and protect Chen Xi for the rest of my life, my eyes watered a bit at the feeling of resolution this evoked in me. We walked out into the yellow backdrop of the Sperrin Mountains. We had a few drinks in front of my Aunt's home, and then we spent the evening at Scarlet's house, before getting the bus back to Dublin. On the bus trip back to Dublin, Chen Xi bemoaned the very modest nature of her wedding day. We spent another month in Dublin, and then we flew to Beijing to be married again.

TEMPLES

Chen Xi and I woke very early from our first sleep in Beijing, and went out for a walk. People were preparing breakfast along the sides of the roads. Chen Xi spoke to a guy seated by towers of steaming bamboo trays, and he brought the top two over to our tiny table. In the trays were *xiaolongbao*, fluffy balls of white. When you put in your chopsticks and pulled one out it peeled away from the others like skin from skin. They were perfectly bite sized, with soft, pre-masticated meat and herbs inside. They hardly needed chewing. There were jars of fried chilli, vinegar and soya sauce on the table, and we each prepared a side dish to dip the *baozi* in. The soft balls absorbed the sauce and spice. There were silhouettes at other tables huddled over noodle bowls. The streetlight traced the steam above these bowls. The streets were bustling and alive even at this early hour.

Waidiren, the migrant workers, were everywhere getting the whole show in motion. When we got back to the apartment Chen Xi's father was setting up breakfast. He poured plastic bags of *dofunaar* into bowls. He was in pyjama bottoms and his torso was bare. There was a bag full of greasy sticks of *youtiao*. Everything was strange and delicious. We were all sweating. Chen Xi's mom had sachets of Nescafe 2+1 for me. I drank this while writing in my diary. They drank soya milk from bowls.

After breakfast, Chen Xi and I went out into the heat haze, the dust, and the relentless whir of cicadas. Chen Xi argued prices with a guy on a motorised rickshaw. We took this to a dusty lot full of *mian bao che*, bread loaf buses. We crowded onto one of these buses as they filled up. Every bus had a couple of guys hustling people in, swinging out from the doors, crying *sanquaiqian*. When a bus was full it took off and raced through its illegal stops.

We went down to the subway at Gu Cheng and got into the train when it pulled to a halt in front of us and the doors whizzed open. We were near the western terminus, so the subway didn't start off crowded, but as we passed Xidan and approached Tian An Men Xi it was completely packed, bodies pressed to one another, hands gripping swinging rails. Before the subway got to Tian An Men, beggars entered the train and pulled themselves up and down through the cars, pleading theatrically for money. There was a beggar with no hands and no legs, and he pulled himself along on a board with wheels under it, using his wrist stumps. He wore only shorts so his leg stumps were visible, scars lined with grime. The beggars had horrible deformities, and they took pains to make these apparent. A beggar would often focus on one person and stick to that person until something was given. I worried that one of them would latch onto me, but they never did. Chen Xi told me that this was because begging from me would make China lose face. We saw a guy in Xidan who had a crowd around him as he kowtowed to the universe, rapping his bloodied forehead repeatedly on the cement with a slow, steady tok tok sound. He was well groomed, and dressed in a shiny black tai chi top. He had a sheet of paper with handwritten Chinese characters beside him, explaining, I guessed, why he was doing this. Nearby a blind guy was playing *erhu*, white, empty eyes staring up at nothing.

We travelled into the city daily, making preparations for the wedding. We got haircuts at a salon run by one of Chen Xi's friends. They played Sarah Brightman and a young lady gave me a head massage. No one had ever done this for me, and she did it with such professionalism. I was moved.

There was a wedding district in Xi Cheng for wedding shops: rings, clothes and photos. I was measured for a suit, and also for a long, traditional Chinese gown in purple, embroidered with golden dragons. When we had the wedding photos taken I expected that I would look very good considering the pains they had taken in costuming us, and posing us in sets in their back rooms. I had even imagined that they might want to hang one of these photos on their wall, as an example of their work. When I saw the photos though I was disappointed by my gawking, avian face. Since I was a boy I have always hated to catch sight of my face in a mirror or a photograph. When Chen Xi's father saw the photos, he said blankly that Chen Xi's face looked like two *da zao*, Chinese dates, on a steamed bun. Our faces had indeed been whitened. Chen Xi was very upset by her father's response to the photos, and she did not let this go for weeks. I would not be surprised to learn that she nurses this grievance till this day.

There were brunches at Seven Uncles' apartment. Fruit was set out in front of golden Buddha statues, and there were framed photos of Chairman Mao on sideboards. The women and children ate together in the living room. Chen Xi's six uncles, her dad, a couple of older cousins and I sat around another table in a small, dark room. They were all shirtless and golden skinned. I sat facing the room from the corner. The women brought in dish after dish of food I did not recognise, pieces of different animals. They would take each dish to their own table when we'd had our fill, and replace it with another. The table was a clutter of bones beside rice bowls. Chen Xi was in the other room, so there was no translation. I couldn't understand a word, but they kept speaking to me as though I could, and I struggled to nod, scowl, smile or laugh at appropriate moments. They drank *bajiu*, and I drank *baijiu* and beer. I knew that I could only get through this if I was pissed. There was a dish with hunks of stringy black meat and I was enjoying it. Seven Uncles called Chen Xi in for translation. He asked me if I knew what this dish was, and then told me it was dog. I told him it was good, but that I wouldn't eat dog. We discussed my reasons for this. They wheeled in the grandfather. He was in an advanced state of neural deterioration, and could only let out hollow groans in response to their words. They had to feed him and he sat across from me in an open pyjama top, food splattered on his chest. They wiped the food from his chest and chin with reverence and respect, as though he were a family relic. I ate bullfrog, deep-fried windpipe, like crunchy Hula Hoops, and shredded jellyfish. I even nibbled at halved duck heads, bill and all. I only drew the line at chicken feet.

Anna Songhurst, Chen Xi's friend and colleague from the Davenport breakfast buffet, and her sister Leah, arrived in Beijing for the wedding. They stayed with us at Chen Xi's family home. Anna was from Bath, studying zoology at Trinity College. She was a creature of positivity and light, and totally alien to me; one of those thoroughly nice people before whom I always feel like such a fraud. She lives in Botswana now, protecting elephants.

My father and his new wife, Netty, arrived from Vancouver. My brother Ralph and his wife, Sam, arrived from Australia. My father's younger brother, Peter, arrived from Botswana. We put my family in the Wan Shan Garden Hotel, the only hotel in Shijingshan that was permitted to take in foreigners.

When we met up in the dark foyer of the hotel we hugged. I cringed and giggled as we pressed our bodies together. Only Peter was too gruff for hugs. He gave me a firm handshake.

I hadn't seen my father since my escape from Calgary, and we almost never talked on the phone. Standing there, facing them, I could see how much he loved and needed Netty. I remembered my mother, from so long ago. I marvelled at how cruel I had been to her when she was dying.

She told us my father had murdered her when he had brought her to Canada. My earliest memories are of my mother's tears. When we left Flin Flon and moved to Calgary we arrived at a new development in Huntington Hills. The lawn was still soil. My mother was crying as we looked around the house, and I asked why. My dad told me it was because she was so happy, but when I looked out at the grey sky, the mud, the snow and the ice, I knew that he was lying.

I don't know what she was hoping for, but it wasn't this. I kicked at a ball of ice by the back porch, trying to free the batgirl trapped inside. She often told us that she could have married a millionaire, a pal of John Chambers, with a mansion near Omagh. When she said this I was always relieved that she hadn't. I protested that then she wouldn't have had me, and she drew me close to her and said she would have had me of course, but I would have had a different father. I was relieved, although I wasn't sure it worked that way.

Now here he was happy as Larry, the perfect husband to Netty. I always felt unbalanced around Netty, as though my subconscious sloshed in its cauldron.

My brother Ralph stood with his arm over Sam's shoulder. He was seven years younger than me. We had been close after our middle brother Deane died, but then we had gone our separate ways. He'd met Sam on a trip through Africa with my father while I was at Trinity. After they'd been married in Australia, Ralph and Sam travelled to Ireland and stayed at Dergmoney while I was in Dublin doing my PhD, and I got to know Sam a bit there. By this time, that stately house was full of hippies. They stayed about a year and then returned to Australia. We had not spoken since he had been in Australia, but I'd called him to tell him I was getting married. Ralph was working for the State of Victoria department of the Environment, helping to protect waterways, and Sam was an architect. Me and my endless dramas made a poor impression on Sam. They were warm, friendly, good-looking people, great at making friends; the type of people who saw right through me.

My uncle Peter lived in Botswana, with his own engineering company, building bridges. He wore a beard, a khaki vest full of pockets, and khaki shorts full of pockets too. He was big and heavy. I hadn't seen Peter since I was three years old, during my first outpouring of memories, when my parents took me from Belfast to stay with my grandparents in Omagh for a week. He was tall and thin then, and so upset that I broke the antenna on his model Stuka up in the attic full of treasures.

Up in the clean, comfortable rooms at Wanshan, with its Western, sit down toilets, Peter showed us photos of his house. He'd designed it in the African style, but with a fortified perimeter. I felt jealous of Peter's house for my father. They had grown up in Glenties, in Donegal, until their father, who was manager of the Ulster Bank in Glenties, became manager of the Ulster Bank in Omagh.

My father hated Omagh. As soon as he finished his degree in geology, he took a job in Tanzania, at the Williamson Diamond Mine. One summer back in Omagh on holiday, he met my mother and married her. He brought her back to Williamson Diamond Mine, and I was born there in 1964.

After I was born my mother insisted that we leave Africa. There were beheadings in the Congo. On the ship back to Ireland my father shot skeet from the bow, and Muriel Hemingway said that I would grow up to be a strong man because I could cry so loud. My father did his PhD at Queens, in Belfast. The troubles were kicking off, and after he completed his doctorate, in 1969, he transplanted us to the oil fields of Canada.

Walking to a *dapaidan* for dinner, after a few drinks in the hotel rooms, I confided in Peter that it was my dream to be a writer. He advised me not to become too excited, because it was an established fact that a Cotter could not do anything great.

The next day, I was fooling around with my father's video camera in Tian An Men Square, and I put it down on a bench beside me before we went into the Forbidden City. As we went into the Forbidden City, he asked for the camera. We ran back to the bench, but there were so many people, of course it was gone. I couldn't say sorry, because I felt that the apology was implicit, and I didn't want to come across as insincere. I felt like such an idiot.

Chen Xi led us on daily pilgrimages to other holy places. Her family rented a van and her brother drove. My family and I had stomach problems from the *dapaidans* and discovered the horror of Chinese public toilets at roadside garages outside of the city. We went to Cheng De, where there are four famous temples. Outside of Beijing the mountain villages were another world. We had trouble finding a place that could take in foreigners. The place we stayed at was so seedy. There was karaoke beneath us, and prostitutes with clients in other rooms. I was revolted and intrigued. I saw my first cockroach, a big one, on the wall above our bed. The next day we hiked up through the ascending levels of wisdom in beautiful temple after temple.

Sitting beside a Nine Dragon Wall with plastic bottles of ice tea, Ralph told me that Sam was pregnant, and that all this walking and climbing in the heat was very difficult for her. They were very grateful to Chen Xi for organising such a full itinerary, but they would need a few days after this to do things at their own speed. When I mentioned this to Chen Xi, she was offended. She had so much planned. We marched on to the Goddess of Infinite Mercy, golden and with a thousand hands, opening out toward me. The statue was huge and we viewed it from a third story balcony, facing her intimately. Each palm had an eye in the centre, meeting mine. The goddess' face was serene. I swooned in the heat. This was the lover of whom I'd dreamed.

On a dry promontory in front of one of these four temples there were guys squatted around a heap of cages holding wild animals. There were songbirds and hawks, hedgehogs, and even a morose porcupine. When Chen Xi explained that you could buy these animals and release them to win favour from the gods, I was affronted by the hypocrisy. She told me not to be, it was *feng sheng,* free life. Peter bought a little yellow bird, and released it when we got to the top of the temple.

On our next excursion we stopped at the Ming Tombs on our way to the great wall. It was a sunny day and I was in a hurry to get to the Great Wall and see it winding into the distance under a clear sky. Chen Xi wanted to linger at the tombs. Once we entered into dispute Chen Xi clammed up and met my objections with a stony face. This provoked me, and while she wanted this seething silence to punish me, I always felt the need to push things toward resolution. I would push harder and harder for her to hear my arguments, and this would eventually set her off into a screaming rage, after which she would descend deeper into silence, making me, in turn, more frantic for her to hear me out, to accept *my* reason. My family witnessed these disputes, and I'm sure they were both ashamed of me and sceptical of the marriage. Chen Xi confided that my father had had a talk with her, and warned her that I could be difficult, that I'd had some bad relationships, and that she should be aware of what she was getting into.

Driving on through the mountains to the Great Wall in silence, we saw a three-wheeled motorbike crushed beneath the wheels of a bus. A guy was standing in the middle of the road, crying and holding up a dead or unconscious person in his arms like a gift to god. I thought about how you are not meant to move a person who might have spinal injuries, and suggested maybe we should stop and tell him this, but Chen Wei drove on. During my time in China, especially the early years, I saw many people slaughtered by vehicles. The driving in Beijing was bad, but outside of Beijing it was the law of the jungle; life was cheap. We went to the Wild Wall, at Mutianyu. We climbed a few hills along the wall, but Sam was too tired to keep going.

After we'd dropped them all off at the hotel, Chen Xi and I went for a beer at Da Yar Li. Chen Xi let me know that in China the husband's family was expected to pay for the wedding ceremony, but because of our special situation her family would pay. She wondered what my family would give us as wedding gifts. We had very little money. After the wedding Chen Wei gave us 5000 RMB that we were able to use to do a bit of travel once my family was gone. I knew that my family would not give wedding gifts, but would consider the price of their flights to join us as gift enough. My uncle Peter left us a 100 USD note, which Chen Xi later spoke of with scorn. I had no idea at this time of the importance of gifts in Chinese culture.

On the morning of our wedding, Chen Xi had friends around to help with her makeup and hair. I had to go out of the apartment and knock on the door until Chen Wei opened a crack, so I could slide through a pink 100 RMB note, which Chen Xi had given me for the purpose. I needed to repeat this a few times before they let me in. I carried Chen Xi in her flouncy white dress across the threshold of the apartment and then down the three flights of stairs. Outside, there was a convoy of black Audis waiting. Chen Xi and I got in the back of Seven Uncles' black Audi and we drove to Wanshan Garden Hotel to collect my family. Then we all went to a nearby restaurant. When we got out of the cars, the younger relatives sprayed Chen Xi and me with plastic foam. We went into the restaurant and were all seated according to a plan. There were speeches and a few songs. My dad went to the front and gave a speech with Chen Xi as his translator. He had with him a world map with China in the centre. He loved maps and found this take on the world to be interesting. He had drawn arrows from the four corners of the world from which we had travelled to China:

from western Canada, Australia, Africa and Northwest Europe. He talked about how China really was the middle kingdom. The Chinese guests loved his speech, and Chen Xi described him as an old gentleman, the kind of man she could fall in love with.

There were costume changes for Chen Xi and me. Chen Xi changed from a white wedding dress to a blue ball gown to a traditional red *chipa*. Her hair was tied up in more and more elaborate coils. I changed from black suit to purple gown. Chen Xi's parents and my dad sat up front and Chen Xi and I approached and bowed deeply before them three times. My dad joked that this was his favourite part of the wedding and I felt ashamed. The food was delicious, with orange prawns that were more like lobsters. Soon after it was served, though, Chen Xi and I had to go around to all of the guests, and I offered each man a cigarette, and lit it for him. Then I would knock back a glass of *baijiu*. Chen Xi unwrapped a sweet for each lady, and placed it in her mouth. When I clicked the lighter to light the cigarettes the men blew out the flame, or turned the cigarettes away in their mouths. Chen Xi urged me not to drink too much, but I argued that it was important to show adequate respect to each guest. I became very jolly, but I didn't become queasy or sick.

My family left a few days after the wedding. We sat outside the KFC near Wanshan Hotel with coffee, and Chen Xi translated her father's speech about how now our two families were joined as one. I felt that my family was a bit sceptical of his honeyed words. Our concepts of family were so different. There were hugs, with which I was uncomfortable, and then they got in the van Chen Xi had organised, and set off for the airport. Netty waved from the back window.

A few days later, Chen Xi, Anna, Leah and I went to Huang Shan, the Yellow Mountain, to see the sun rise over the Sea of Clouds. The train station was overwhelming. I had never seen so many people gathered in one place. It was wretched and chaotic. Migrant workers squatted everywhere, or sat on their chequered bags eating little tubs of instant noodles. There were no lineups in front of the ticket booths, only surging mobs. Chen Xi pushed to the front of the mob to purchase tickets, pushing her arm through the little window, with money in her hand, and then we forced ourselves through a mass of people to get onto the train. We had soft sleepers, two sets of bunk beds in a single compartment, but when we found this compartment there were families sitting on the beds eating instant noodles and pink sausages. I had expected Chen Xi to chase them away, but I discovered that this was just the way things worked. We found spaces on the beds between the three generations of unwanted guests.

As we travelled south from Beijing, I despaired looking out at the squalid, industrialised landscape. Every riverbed was dry, and there were mountains with sides gouged out of them. From every fence post, and from every twig on every skinny tree, shreds of white plastic fluttered. When we got to Huang Shan, we spent half a day hiking to the top. As we progressed, Chen Xi read out the placards to us, giving a name to every rock formation and ancient, stunted tree. Every flight of stairs carved into the mountain also had a placard with its name, and number of steps. When we got to the top of the mountain I discovered that I needed to stay in a separate building from the girls. I went on my own into a room in which a bunch of young Chinese guys were playing cards, drinking beer and eating sunflower seeds. I tried to communicate with them, but they had no English. I lay down on my bed, but I have always been a light sleeper, and they played cards until the early hours.

Chen Xi got me up early, before sunrise, and we joined a pilgrimage of people making their way to the highest peak, from which we could witness the sun rising over the Sea of Clouds. There was standing room only on this peak, and we struggled to find an ideal spot to witness the sunrise. When the sun did rise, it smeared red and orange light across the miles of cloud beneath us. People scurried to ledges to get photographs.

When the spectacle subsided we made our way back to our rooms and gathered our things before hiking back down the mountain. There were wiry young local guys sprinting up and down the mountain paths in pairs with poles on their shoulders toting bags of groceries. Four guys carried a fat guy up the mountain on a litter. He sat up on the bier with an expression of studied arrogance, and his family gathered round taking photos of him. On the train back to Beijing,

Chen Xi and I squabbled a lot, and I felt embarrassed that Anna and Leah were witnessing this. Chen Xi was so sweet with Anna and Leah; it was only with me that there was all this friction. Anna and Leah left Beijing a few days later.

My favourite thing about Beijing was the *dapaidans*. They were everywhere, places where you could sit outside and have a beer and a bite to eat, but the biggest local *dapaidan* was at Da Yar Li, the Big Pear. Every afternoon they set out about twenty plastic tables in the space in front of the two stone lions. Around the tables were trays of food. There were so many things to choose from: spicy crayfish, snails, duck heads and necks, beans, tofu, tripe, fish large and small. We drank beer and ate peanuts boiled in spices, and hairy beans which Chen Wei taught me to shoot into my mouth by pinching the pod. *Yuangroutrau'r*, little skewers of barbecued lamb sprinkled with cumin and chilli, were the stars of the show, and I loved to see the waitress bringing over a handful of twenty of these. We drank beer and pulled the meat from the sticks with our teeth. Chen Xi and I would sit with Chen Wei and his girlfriend Yang Yang until late into the evening. Chen Wei had learned how to say I love China, and he sat up and repeated this frequently, sinking back into his chair with satisfaction. Chen Xi's extended family had pictures of Mao Tse Deng in their cars and in their homes, and he was sacred and irreproachable. When I questioned their devotion to Mao Tse Deng, Chen Xi would become cross, and she wouldn't translate for me. She told me only that he was the father of modern China.

I could not understand how people could so blindly love their country; I felt it was important to be critical of your government. I tried to debate Chen Wei's love of China with the help of Chen Xi's translation. This usually became a debate between Chen Xi and me. As for Chen Wei, his love of China was sincere, unconsidered and absolute. Chen Xi told me that China needed a strict and powerful government, because with so many people it was prone to chaos. Chen Xi had visited Tian An Men on the day before the crackdown, but only to witness the spirit of festivity. She knew people who had disappeared after that day, but she felt that it was their own fault for causing trouble.

Chen Xi told me that the government made it rain in Beijing. I was sceptical, but we would often hear cannons in the mountains to the west as they seeded the clouds before a downpour. When it started to rain, the staff at Da Yar Li brought out umbrellas and inserted them in holes in the centres of the plastic tables. Once we ran home through the rain and thunder and Chen Xi was laughing as we were soaked to the skin. I watched her as she ran and laughed and felt so happy that she was my wife, that this hilarity was my life.

On the evening Beijing won its Olympic bid, we were at the *dapaidan* in front of Da Yar Li. They had set up a television among the trays of food and everyone watched this while I focussed on my *pijiou* and *yangyoutra'r*. For the Chinese, winning the Olympic bid was an important point of honour.

They wanted to see China recognised and respected. When it was announced that China had won its bid to host the 2008 Olympics, Chen Wei lifted his arms over his head and howled *wo ai ni Zhong Guo*. Fireworks began to go off at all corners, and people flooded onto the streets to celebrate. Anyone with a little bit of English approached me and said welcome to Beijing. They held up children in crotchless jammies toward me, to say hello, to be blessed by my gaze, as envoy from the outside world. They told me how proud they were of China. I had never witnessed such enthusiasm.

A few days later we were at an aunt's apartment. I had a sore back and an uncle was giving me a massage as I sat in a chair watching TV. I fainted from the heat and the pressure of the massage. Someone on the news was saying that Beijing would now focus on raising the English level of its people, in preparation for its hosting of the games. Chen Xi told me that this had been all over the news recently, and that when the government set its mind to something like this, it would happen. She told me about Maple Leaf International School, where Chinese people would do the Canadian high school diploma. We decided to return to Beijing in six months, and set up a school to run the Irish Leaving Cert. A few days later, we were back in Dublin.

A BIDNIZ MAN

As soon as we were back in our flat on Beechwood Avenue, I called Des and Carl. We met up in McSorley's, around the corner on Ranelagh Road, and I became a businessman, all fraud, comedy and farce. I drank Drambuie with ice clinking ostentatiously. I invited them to be our business partners. They were enthusiastic. We were all convinced we would be rich.

I felt like a new man. I had focus and hope. I quit smoking, and renounced my aspiration to save everything from dying with my writing. Everything would be OK, if there was lots of money. I had come to this understanding very late in the game, but I intended to make up for time lost. I had been working days and evenings just to pay the rent, and I knew that this would be the story of my life unless I made a break and found some new direction. Chen Xi liked to walk down

Beechwood Avenue in the evenings, looking into the lovely terraced houses, admiring the gardens, speculating what it would be like to live in such a house. I knew that if I worked for a hundred years as an ESL teacher in Dublin, I could never afford to buy us one of these houses. I gripped onto the idea of a school in China as though my life depended on it.

Things were going better for Chen Xi and me. Chen Xi did work placement for her final term at Griffith College. She worked as receptionist at a hip advertising agency, Chemistry, which was only a short walk away, off Leeson Square. The lads had fun with her. Someone kept phoning and asking for Elvis. She would look for Elvis and they would tell her he was in another room. Then someone would tell her he had left the building. When she became confused about this, and confided in me, I explained to her what was going on. She tried not to show it, but I could tell she was offended.

I finished the summer working at Swan Training, teaching groups of Italian and Austrian teenagers. In September I gave this up, as Des got me a job in Old Bawn, a secondary school in Tallaght. I had no certification to teach in a public school but I managed to get the job because I had a PhD, and they had no one else to do it. I was the home teacher for a group of final year Applied Leaving Cert students. They were a squad of loveable rogues. I was straight and open with them, and we got along well. I called them the SweatHogs, though they didn't get the reference. I taught them

"They fuck us up our moms and dads," and they were right with me. There was a rolling teacher's strike toward the end of my time at Old Bawn and I spent a few days a week sitting with the other teachers doing nothing.

Once, I looked out the window and saw the headmaster at the gates, where the kids had congregated. Every time he turned to come back into the school grounds, they threw plastic bottles at him. I went out and watched his back while he got into the school. One of my students kicked a soccer ball at him, and I took it and threw it into some bushes. The next time we were in class the kid who had kicked the ball told me that they were all disappointed, because they'd thought I was cool. The hard feelings didn't last long though, and in the end they gave me a bottle of whiskey and a little stash box with a stylised marijuana leaf on the lid as a going-away gift.

On Sundays Des came around to help me edit my book on Joyce. I had done two revisions for Cambridge University Press, but had given up on this. I exchanged emails with Greg Lainsbury, who had been my comrade in creative writing classes with Chris Wiseman and Aritha Van Herk at the University of Calgary. He told me that he'd had his PhD thesis on Raymond Carver published by Routledge in "a series of outstanding dissertations." I wrote to Routledge, and they agreed to publish my book on Joyce. Des and I spent our Sunday afternoons polishing it up before I sent a final version to them. When I sent the book off, I said goodbye to all that. I knew that nothing would come of the book, and that I would never find work as an academic. I didn't have the talent, plain and simple. As a businessman who had given up smoking, I recognised that it was all waffle anyway. *Joyce and the Perverse Ideal*, what a joke. I would get all the gold and silver that I could, animate the trivial days and ram them with sun. No more of the moody-broody, I would instead demonstrate sheer strength of will. I began listening to Pink Floyd, *Animals*, again. It had been my first album when I was twelve. Now I identified with the dogs.

I watched the delicate line of Chen Xi's eyelash as she slept. I felt protective of her, and committed to our future. One evening we watched a TV show about young people in Ibiza, while dipping shreds of roast duck in Hoisin sauce from the coffee table in front of the sofa, and wrapping it with cucumber and spring onion cut in thin strips. Chen Xi warned me that the girls in China could be very cunning, and that they would try to seduce me. She told me that she didn't want to go back to China if it meant that she would lose her marriage. I assured her that this wouldn't happen. I felt that, given the nature of my perversity, I might find a woman who would hurt me, but I would not find another woman with whom I could strive together, as an ally. She would have no competition. Sex, for me, precluded love.

As the time approached for our departure, I realised that we needed investment. Carl and Des wanted to be equal partners in the venture, but neither had cash or were willing to travel to China. I approached the owners of Swan Training, and Chen Xi and I met them in a pub in Ranelagh. Oliver and Michael were successful businessmen who had built up a strong school on Grafton Street. They were intelligent and humorous, and they balanced one another well. Oliver was responsible for the academic side of things, and Michael looked after the money. Michael's mantra was bums on seats. I was full of confidence and enthusiasm when I pitched our idea for a school in Beijing to them. I showed them my speculative cash projections done up in Excel. Michael said he was impressed by the fire in me, and he felt that if anyone could pull it off it would be me. They agreed to go into partnership with us. My teaching at Old Bawn was finished for Christmas break and Michael and Oliver gave Chen Xi and me some administrative work at Swan. I was able to deal with the group leaders of our students quite well, but it was more difficult to deal with the Irish teachers. They didn't like to see me come out of nowhere and assume a position of authority over them. I had some money now, and I bought a leather trench coat, a pair of yellow cords, a nice zip-up jumper and a cool pair of leather winklepickers.

In his research Carl discovered that the Irish Leaving Certificate was being run in Libya. I managed to get an appointment to speak with a Minister in the Dáil, and Oliver accompanied me. I asked the Minister for permission to run the Irish leaving Certificate in China. He was friendly and polite, although he no doubt recognised that I was a loose cannon. I pointed out that the Leaving Cert was being run in

Libya, and although I didn't say it I tried to imply that this was probably a grey area on which the Irish government might not want light shone. There had been shipments of arms to the IRA from Libya. The Minister left it that if I could get set up in China, I could call back and we would look at the Leaving Cert again. I was happy enough with the outcome of the meeting, although I was a bit ashamed of how out of my depth I had been in speaking to this man.

Chen Xi and I made business cards for the Sino-Irish Education Group. I was Academic Director, and Chen XI was CEO. Christmas was coming and we would be leaving for China on January 2nd. On the walk back from the Business Registration Office we stopped at Swan Training on Grafton Street, and I asked Oliver to give us some startup money. We signed a contract dividing the business four ways. Oliver passed me 20,000 USD in an envelope. That evening we called Carl and Des over, and I told them we had received money from Swan. When they asked me what their positions were now I avoided giving them a direct answer. I told them that we needed money to start the business, and that they wouldn't be able to help us much without coming to China. Chen Xi and I had been close with Carl and Des, and I was sorry that we had to hurt them in this way.

The evening before we left for China, I was crossing the road to go to the Spar around the corner from us, and a guy with floppy blonde hair in a beautiful blue convertible nudged me with his car because the lights had changed while I was crossing. Before I had a chance to think I mule-kicked the door of his car. He drove on around the corner. When I came out of the shop, I looked around for him, and made sure no one was watching as I went back to our flat. I felt so much pressure. During the past few weeks I'd had a few standoffs with drunk guys on the road. I was afraid that I wouldn't be able to make it out of Ireland without getting into some sort of trouble with the law, and I knew I needed to escape.

Chen Xi and I travelled back to Beijing on January 2nd, 2002. It was the same day that Ireland switched to the euro, so we travelled with this new currency in our pockets. I wore my leather trench coat, my yellow cords and my winklepickers. I had 20,000 USD in a money belt under my new jumper. At the airport, we discovered that our bags were way too heavy. Chen Xi was thumping my back as we pulled things out of our luggage and discarded them. I left the leather trousers I had found in Eileen's apartment from a boyfriend before me, books and folders full of notes, Chinese tea, and some of Chen Xi's clothes, which was when the thumping started. It was such a risk. We were giving up all we had grafted to gather. I felt confident though that whatever befell us in China it could not be worse than the small, hopeless life that we'd been living in the sweepings of Dublin.

When our connecting flight was delayed in Amsterdam because of snow in Beijing, we were taken with the other passengers by shuttle bus to a hotel in Amsterdam. Once we were settled in the room, we got a cab into the city, and found a coffee shop that sold weed. I got a big reefer of turbo skunk, and smoked half of it down before I was hit by an excruciating dose of paranoia. We went out onto the street, and started walking. I noticed other people dressed in casual clothes, and felt out of place in my leather trench coat and yellow cords. A black guy in an oversized tweed cap, who had been singing to passersby, latched onto me and followed me along, circling around me begging for money. I felt the money bag with Swan's investment bouncing on my belly under my jumper, and I felt like such a fool. This wasn't me. I felt such horror in becoming someone I'd never been. We called over a cab and I dived into the back seat. Chen Xi got into the front seat, and on the drive back to the hotel the Arab driver flirted with her, while I was the cowardly lion in the back seat, in yellow cords and winkle pickers. This shame was turned on its head, into arousal. When we got back to the hotel I tried to talk to her about this, but she only listened, saying nothing. When I pressed her for a response, she said that it didn't seem realistic to her, then we went to sleep. I finished the remains of the turbo skunk reefer the next morning before we got on the shuttle-bus back to the airport, and continued on to Beijing.

Seven Uncles met us at the airport with his secretary, who was dressed in red. Chen Xi described her as his little wife. I wanted one too, and with lots of money I knew I could have one some day. She was beautiful and inert. It was an open secret that Seven Uncles had a little wife, and his real wife, the mother of his son, just had to accept this. He drove us along the 5th Ring Road, to Chen Xi's parents' house. Beijing was different in the winter. It was drab and grey, and there were patches of carbon-dusted snow along the sides of the roads. I had hoped to go to the *dapaidan* at Da Yar Li as soon as we arrived, but was disappointed to learn that in winter it wasn't open.

We only stayed with Chen Xi's family a couple of weeks before we moved into a new development in Sihui Dong. Sihui Dong was the eastern terminus of Line One of the Beijing underground, the east-west line, which runs along Chang An Jie, and bisects Tian An Men Square and the Forbidden City at its centre. We moved to Sihui Dong because the east of Beijing is the international business district, and that was where we initially saw our market. Beijing was so clearly zoned. Chaoyang was the Central Business District, and it held the embassies and international businesses. Most of Beijing's wealth was concentrated there. Haidian, beginning at the northwest corner of Line Two of the underground, was the university district, and almost all foreign people lived in one of these two districts.

Shijingshan was another world, and until I started bringing foreign teachers in, I never saw another foreign face there. It was convenient for us to get from Sihui Dong to Chaoyang, where the foreigners were concentrated. We took Line One a few stations west to Jianguomen, then transferred to Line Two, and travelled a couple of stations north. Back then there were only two lines, while now there are twenty or so.

Line Two, the loop-line, ran around the Second Ring Road, at the centre of which was Tian An Men Square, and the portrait of Mao above the gates of the Forbidden City. The embassy district, foreign bars and nightclubs were in Chaoyang, to the east of the Forbidden City. We introduced ourselves at the Irish Embassy, and handed out our Sino-Irish Education Group business cards. Everyone was too polite to ask us what we meant by Group. They could recognise my audacity in a way that the Chinese could not. We went to a few functions at the embassy, and continued to distribute our Sino-Irish Education Group business cards.

At a coffee shop near Silk Street, which in those days consisted of carts in an alleyway, and not a shopping plaza, I discovered *That's Beijing*, a weekly events magazine in English. I did a reconnaissance mission to Maggie's Bar, which specialised in Mongolian prostitutes. Maggie's Bar was managed by the Chinese government, to ensure that foreigners in Beijing would not run amok among Chinese women. The bouncers were undercover police, so it never felt dangerous to me; instead it felt warm, friendly and hilarious. There was a hot-dog stand out front, with crispy onions and sauerkraut.

Maggie's was sometimes referred to as the Mongolian Embassy. I got a phone number one evening before going home. The next day I showed a text message to a taxi driver and he dropped me off at an apartment full of Mongolian girls. There I found myself lying naked on the coffee table, surrounded by these fully clothed girls, laughing and touching me with the hundreds of hands of the Goddess of Infinite Mercy, soft lashes blinking in their palms.

Chen Xi and I attended day-long meetings in Haidian and Chaoyang, and in strange, isolated campuses on the outskirts of Beijing. These were rigid worlds all their own, run in a military style. In the foyers hung portraits of Marx, Lenin, Stalin and Mao. Crystal doorknobs waggled loosely. These meetings would last full days, and often consecutive days. I sat beside Chen Xi across a large, gleaming table from a team of Chinese business people. I would smile and nod sagely as they spoke in Chinese, and when Chen Xi translated for me, I offered up some reply or suggestion. I told them we could do anything.

I watched a guy sneak away to a corner for a cigarette, and it seemed like such a great way to escape the meetings for a while. A couple of days later I was smoking again. This made it much easier for me to socialise with the people in these meetings. Cigarettes, and then beer and *baijiu*, became the common ground on which I was able to communicate with Chinese people. We would laugh at ourselves glancing at our packs of cigarettes, which now sat on the tables during the meetings. The best parts of the meetings were in the stairwells, before we moved to a restaurant for a great meal, beer and *baijiu*. I found that a jolly and happy persona was much more attractive to the Chinese than a serious business head.

While we were attending meetings in the east of Beijing, Chen Xi's mother was busy setting up meetings for us in Shijingshan. She introduced us to an old and distinguished gentleman, Teacher John, an English teacher at the Agricultural University in Haidian. His English wasn't great, but he spoke in a slow and measured way, and he exuded an aura of wisdom. A survivor of the cultural revolution, he often spoke about the Iron Rice Bowl.

Teacher John set us up a meeting with government leaders in Daxing district. Daxing is a surreal agricultural zone to the south of Shijingshan. It is famous for watermelons, some of which are grown as cubes for ease of stacking. This district was even more Chinese, and less Beijing, than Shijingshan. It was a straight drive south for about an hour from Shijingshan, across massive bridges over dried-out river beds, a dusty world of walled concrete compounds.

We spent a morning with Mr Chen and Mr Wang in a meeting room around a huge, gleaming oval table, and then we got in a small bus with curtains and moved to a restaurant, where we were led into an exquisite private room. Their driver sat by the door, and waitresses stood around the table silently. Chen and Wang ordered the most impressive dishes on the menu, and a couple of bottles of the best *baijiu*, Maotai. Chen Xi whispered to me to be careful, but I was never careful with Mr Chen and Mr Wang. I *ganbie'd* with them individually, and enthusiastically. I even *ganbie'd* with the waitresses. They praised my ability to drink. We met them daily for the same routine. I managed to get through the shots by chasing them with beer. Neither Chen nor Wang did this. At the end of the week while I sat utterly pissed, Chen Xi signed a three year contract for us to provide training to all of the Public School English teachers in Da Xing. Starting in September we would be running five concurrent classes in Da Xing, three mornings a week. I needed to hire teachers, and prepare course material.

At the same time that we were dealing with the guys at Da Xing, Chen Xi's father was introducing us to people in the Shijingshan Education Department, and to the headmasters of various public schools in Shijingshan District. These meetings always ended with a trip to a restaurant, but compared to Chen and Wang, these guys were lightweights when it came to the drinking.

Swan sent over Peter and Andrew, and we did demo classes in schools and at community centres. We rented an office and four classrooms in Zhongchu Daxia, on Chang An Jie, right beside the Bajiou Youleyaun subway station. We hired a receptionist, and a sales person. Andrew and Peter were our teachers, I was our Academic Director, Chen Xi was our CEO, and Chen Xi's father became Marketing Manager and Assistant Headmaster. No longer in long johns, he wore suit and tie.

When Oliver and Michael visited from Swan they stayed at Jianguo Hotel in east Beijing, to deal with agents recruiting summer students for Swan. They were not willing to take the subway to our school in Zhongchu Daxia. Instead we took a cab, and on the way I pointed out the endless residential buildings and told them that in each of these apartments were one-child families who wanted their kid to learn English. Bums on seats, I kept saying, and rubbing my hands together. Michael and Oliver were impressed with the office and the classrooms, and over dinner in Jianguomen they agreed to invest more money.

I walked up and down Changanjie carrying red banners with our Chinese staff. I joked around with all the people that I saw. There was a lot of interest. Beijing was gearing up for the Olympics. The slogan was One World, One Dream. Everywhere we went Chinese people came over and said Welcome to Beijing. Beijing was focussed on opening up to the world, and becoming an international city. It was a great time to be *laowai*.

AIHUA / 爱华

After Chen Xi and I returned to Beijing in Jan 2002, we spent a few months in meetings in the east of Beijing, trying to find a company big enough to join us in our project. To be eligible to be registered as a joint venture, we were required to allow the Chinese government to lock a few million RMB in a secure account. This was well beyond our means. We had hoped to be established as a joint venture, though, because this would give us the right to employ foreign teachers, and enable me to hold legal standing in the company.

Toward the end of spring 2002, Chen Xi signed a contract with Daxing Education Board to provide foreign teacher training to their public school teachers, and we had agreements to provide English lessons by foreign teachers to children in three Shijingshan primary schools. The Daxing teacher training, and the teaching in primary schools, would begin in September, at the start of the next school year. In May of 2002, we opened our first centre.

Chen Xi was wrestling with regulations, but to me it seemed like the wild west. We decided to just set up and get started. Everywhere I went people smiled and welcomed me. They wanted me to speak with their children. Beijing was gearing up for the Olympics, and the people were enthusiastic to see their city take its place on the world stage. The government had ordained that the people of Beijing should welcome the world to the 2008 Olympics with good English, and the people were happy with this. They saw ahead a world of international business and cultural exchange.

I had determined that confidence was the secret to being a successful businessman. There were so many buildings full of one-child families who wanted that child to learn English. Everyone knew that the English teachers in the public schools didn't speak very good English. They could explain grammar in an authoritative tone, and teach students to pass specific exams, but that was all. Foreign teachers, on the other hand, were glamorous, worldly and modern.

Chen Xi's family were well-connected in Shijingshan and at this time everything worked through webs of connection: *guanxi*. Chen Xi took a business licence in her name. I was on a spousal visa, but according to Chinese regulations I could have no legal standing in a Chinese business. I knew that I could trust Chen Xi, but the honorary and theoretical status of my ownership of Aihua made me sensitive about being treated with respect by our Chinese staff. Most Chinese people seemed gentle and gracious, courteous to the point of deference. In my head I had to balance this against the many stories of Chinese owners removing foreign partners once the business got up and running.

Our first centre was in an office building managed by the local government, Zhongchu Daxia. Above the entry was the crest of the Chinese Communist party. The building was on Changanjie, beside the north-west exit of the Bajiou Youleyuan subway station. Across Changanjie was the Shijingshan Hospital. Changanjie was barricaded along its length, except at intersections, so that people could not cross on foot except at designated crossings. There was a footbridge across Changanjie here, and from this bridge you could see the mountains to the west of Beijing, and to the east, on a blue sky day, you could make out the towers of Guomao on the other side of Beijing. To the east of the hospital, on the south side of Changanjie, was a construction site for a new residential development, Jie Shi Ping, which would be two tower blocks of twenty four stories, much higher than the other residential buildings in the area. There were to be western style toilets in these new buildings. To the east of this was Hualian Shopping Centre and the Wanshan Garden Hotel.

To the west along Changanjie, after the underpass of the 5th Ring Road, was the Bajiou amusement park. To the south of the amusement park was Shijingshan Tiyuguan, the sports stadium. Behind us, to the north, was Lao Shan, which at this time of year was pink with cherry blossom. They were turning these hills into the Olympic mountain bike track, and they were building the Olympic velodrome beside them. Next to our building were three restaurants and a KTV. In the evenings there were dapaidans in front of these. There were crowds flowing in and out of the subway station, and illegal taxi drivers hustling people into their cars. Once, the police grabbed a peasant selling DVDs at the subway entrance by the back of his hair and frog marched him into their car. I saw a little girl who had been hurt and sent out to beg, sitting alone howling in the centre of the sidewalk.

You entered Zhongchudaxia under the crest of the communist party into a foyer with black marble tiles on floors and walls, two elevators on one side and a stairwell on the other. The interior of the elevators were mirrored. They were always busy, and someone was always left behind. If you got in you were pressed tightly to other people. We were only on the third floor, so I preferred to take the stairs. In fact, the stairwell became my office, where I would smoke and drink Nescafe 2+1.

We set up a reception desk in the foyer between the elevator and the stairwell. We had two small rooms and two large rooms down the hall to the east. The building was mostly occupied by trading businesses. We used one of the small rooms as our office, and set the other three up as classrooms.

Three of the public schools into which we would be sending foreign teachers in September were near Gucheng, the next subway station to the west. Number two and six primary schools were ours, as well as Gucheng Middle School. Our other school was Ping Er Xue Xiao, which was past the western terminus of the Beijing underground, in Pinguoyuar, where the mountains began, and where Beijing became part mountain village.

These schools were all tucked among gated communities: *xiao chu*. All of the residential areas in Beijing are closed communities, with formidable walls around them. The gates are manned by *bao an*, security guards in a standard China-wide uniform. When I first arrived in China I thought they were police. These *bao an* were mostly *waidiren*, poor and uneducated. You could not enter or exit any community except through these monitored gates. Some *xiao chu* had gardens and public spaces, but most had only car parks.

The schools were also behind high walls and with *bao an* at the gates. They were large, composed of a few five story buildings. There was always a rubberised area outside for the children to run around, or, more often, do callisthenics in ranks, or stand at attention for the ceremonial raising and lowering of the flag, and shrill speeches from the headmaster. If foreign teachers and I walked past while they were doing callisthenics or standing at attention, the kids would crane their necks to watch us, until their teachers lay into them. At one of the first schools I visited, a kid poked his head out of a third story window and called out hello, hello until a teacher appeared and thumped him repeatedly on the back of the head as she pulled him away from the window. You had to feel sorry for the kids, caught in these people-making machines.

The kids all wore tracksuit uniforms, with different colours and designs for different schools, mainly pastel greens, blues and pinks. Some kids wore the red scarf of the Young Pioneers. Some had badges of merit pinned to an arm of their tracksuits. The insides of the schools were clean and bright. There were long halls of classrooms on either side. The classes were of about forty students, and the public school teachers were frazzled and cranky.

Some kids had small, dry beans taped to points on their ears to stimulate pressure points, a type of auriculotherapy based on the same general principles as acupuncture. Ear seeds were placed on certain points, usually along meridian lines, to help clear up any qi blockages. Other kids had a white plaster over one lens of their glasses; some had small protuberances of flesh at their ears, like aborted attempts at extra earlobes. After each class, there was gentle music and the kids put down their things and gave themselves eye and face massages, to the melodious instructions of the pre-recorded voice on the intercom system. I felt privileged to be in a position to come and go freely in these schools, as though I had been allowed access behind the curtain.

The kids could be rambunctious, but this was only blowing off steam, it was not a question of rebellion, and they were never disrespectful to teachers or elders. The school day ran from eight in the morning to five in the evening, even for the youngest children. With more traditional teachers they were expected to sit erect the entire time, with their arms folded out in front of them, parallel to their thighs. The kids were under huge pressure to do well in school, because there was so much competition for university places. Beijing kids had an advantage, but there were no guarantees. The teaching style was all just preparation for exams. There was no debating perspectives or raising queries or objections, the right answers had all been decided. It was commonly accepted among both parents and educators that this education style did not encourage creative thinking, but as with many such issues, they felt that although this was a pity, given the special circumstances of China's massive population, there was no other way. When they got home, the kids, even the youngest, did homework until ten in the evening. The parents squeezed private training into any free time they could find. The kids were doing private art, music, maths, calligraphy, even Go and lego classes after school and at weekends. Now, they also had my school as a choice.

When I started sending teachers foreign teachers into public schools, they taught classes of forty, and only the most dedicated of public school English teachers would stay in the classrooms with us. We found the kids already had English names often based on a theme, such as colour. With forty students in a class we found the names had been duplicated, with, for example, Blue One, Blue Two, and Blue Three.

The kids who came to our centre tended to have more weirdly-impressive names, such as Treasure, Boxer, Veronica, and Ice Dragon. The first parents who signed their kids up at our centre were doctors and nurses from the hospital across the road, teachers from the local schools, and government people. They often had some English, and while their kids were in class they stayed around the school and chatted with me. They were intelligent and responsible people, and I learned from them what they hoped we could do for their children. I felt honoured to have been entrusted with the education of their children.

Chen Xi had a very clear idea of how we should structure our staff. We would have an Administration Department, a Sales and Marketing Department, and a Teaching Department. Most of the people Chen XI hired were family connections, who spoke no English. Chen Xi was in charge of the Administration Department, which consisted of Accounts, IT, and a driver. We bought a van with nine seats. We had stickers put on this van with our logo, our phone number and Chinese slogans. At the front was the Irish flag. It was put on backwards though, and the orange was more like red, so that it was actually the Italian flag. The driver was a friend of Chen Xi's father. Chen Xi's brother, Chen Wei, set up our twelve computers, and networked them. Chen Wei's wife, Yang Yang, was our accountant.

Chen Xi's way of dealing with our staff was very harsh. She would get angry at any incompetence, and berate whoever was in front of her as they bowed their heads in supplication. When I tried to speak to her about this, she told me this is how it is done in China, and that you need to be strict with Chinese people or they will take advantage of you. I saw that this was how the Chinese public school teachers spoke to children, and how people treated waitresses. She was unable to control her anger. Chen Wei and Yang Yang left within a couple of weeks because of the way Chen Xi spoke to them. We replaced them with Cathy and one of Chen Wei's buddies, Fan Cheng.

I tried to pay attention to accounts, but they were all in Chinese, and full of gifts and special cases. Chen Xi became impatient when I asked her to talk me through them. In fairness we were very busy, but she was the only one with English so there was no one else I could ask.

Chen Xi's father was in charge of the Sales and Marketing Department. He became known as Chen Fu, assistant leader Chen, and he is known as that to this day, long after we have finished with Aihua. Chen Fu became more and more central to our business. We couldn't have done it without him. He found and negotiated the rent for our site in Zhongchudaxia. He proposed the name Aihua, which means love China, and also Ireland-China.

His department consisted of the two young ladies who sat at the reception desk. Tian Ning was Yang Yang's friend. She was very beautiful, but she was not submissive enough with the customers. Chen Xi was hard on her, and hounded her out after a couple of years. Chen Xi's mother introduced us to Ainsley, who was smart, small and plain. She had a bit of English, and I was mostly able to learn from her what was going on with the school.

At first Chen Fu hung red banners with our name on them out our windows at Zhongchudaxia. Then, we set up billboards all around Shijingshan, at subway stations, bus stops, and above department stores. I would discover new ones wherever I went. At first these billboards only had a red background with our name and telephone number, in exploding yellow characters, but later, when I became involved in the design, they became more elaborate.

The students for our off site programs needed to pay for our classes. The headmasters got a cut and we got the lion's portion. To encourage students to pay for our classes, we were permitted to do promotions inside the schools. Chen Fu organised meals with headmasters and their staff. I would stand up and give a speech in English to headmasters and teachers seated around dinner tables full of beer and *baijiou*.

I would wing it. Chen Xi stood beside me translating after each sentence or two. She was always trying to slow me down, and I laughed at her protests and sipped my beer. I would talk about our teachers, and why it was helpful for their children to learn English from native speakers. I talked about One World, One Dream, and the advantages of learning languages at a young age. I pictured a world in which all nations were as one, and it seemed easy enough to believe this back then.

I did demo classes to groups of children in front of parents and teachers assembled in many-tiered auditoriums, leading a string of disorientated foreign teachers to sit on display in a line at the front. The headmasters, and then Chen Fu, and then Chen Xi, would each give a long speech, while the parents and children gawked at the foreign teachers, who sat upright fidgeting, lost and dismayed, our team of dancing monkeys. Monkey King, I was called up to a round of applause to teach a pre-selected group of kids with an enthusiasm that had me dripping with sweat. Occasionally, I had the chance to shout, You! Yes you, laddy! You behind the striped shirt. The kids loved this kind of shtick, and it broke the ice. I always had the student I spoke to stand. You boy, I would bark at some sweet, grinning kid, how many ears do you have? And when the kid replied I have seven years, I would run to the chalkboard and draw a head with seven ears, repeating incredulously seven ears? The boy has seven ears? Can it be?

I would ask them to show me monkey, dog, elephant, and chicken. I learned that there are formal ways of enacting these animals in China, and that these animals made different sounds in Chinese than they did in English. Next we would work on what monkeys, dogs, cows and chickens like to eat, all roaring out together monkeys like to eat bananas. There was always a question as to whether monkeys preferred bananas or peaches. Pigs definitely loved watermelon peels, and mice loved rice, there was a popular Chinese song to prove it

I was in charge of the Teaching Department, and there were so many things that needed to be decided. The problem of teaching material was largely taken out of our hands by the fact that the schools wanted to use the Cambridge Young Learners program. This was the exam standard, and a lot of kids prepared to do the annual Cambridge Young Learners' Exam. Though the art was poor, and there was no teaching system, only pages of animals, colours, clothes, family members, vehicles, etc, they had the market sewn up, and there was a lot of money involved, with most kids in China buying copies of their books. We stuck with Cambridge Young Learners for a couple of years, and then changed material because we felt we needed to differentiate our onsite program from our offsite program.

Our onsite and offsite classes ran for one term each, and we completed one level of Cambridge Young Learners per term. In terms of teaching speed this meant that our teachers needed to spend 45 minutes working on a two page spread of nothing but labelled bubbles of colours, for example, and nothing more. For on-site classes, they needed to run two 45 minute periods on such material. I was always having to rein in the teachers, some of whom were completing four or five units in a single period.

We hired a few students with a little bit of English from the college Chen Xi's mother worked at, to travel in the school bus with the foreign teachers, and lead them into the public schools. When they were not with the foreign teachers we sent them out to distribute flyers.

There were so many factors to consider. Chen Xi, Chen Fu and I were cracking up.

We hired Grace Pan as General Manager, and Jackie Yao as Director of Studies. Jackie looked like a smiling Buddha, and he was a floridly traditional Chinese man. Grace was tall and vigorous. She had worked as a manager at the Swiss Hotel in Chaoyang. She was dating the Head Chef there, a German guy. I saw a taunting sexuality behind her strict and efficient business manner. Jackie worked better with Chen Xi, and Grace worked better with me.

There were long meetings where Chen Fu and I chain smoked while Chen Xi had asthma attacks and roared at us to open the windows. Other staff members wheezed meekly, in case Chen XI might set into one of them by default. After the meetings we opened the windows before students arrived.

As that first September approached, and we prepared for Daxing teacher training, and offsite programs at the local public school, the pressing concern was where were the foreign teachers who would teach these classes?

Peter and Andrew arrived from Swan Training in May, and they helped with demo classes, and walked with me past the subway stations holding open our red banners. I had no idea how to hire foreign teachers, and I was lucky that a friend from Trinity put me in touch with Yvonne, Kara and Kieth. Oliver interviewed them at Swan, and signed contracts. They were with us by June, on tourist visas. We put them into apartments in Pinguoyuar. They were the kind of teachers that Aihua became known for in Shijingshan. They were recently out of college, pleasant looking, and good natured. They were flexible, and they had fun with the kids. They helped me develop a roaring-chorusing call and response technique that was to become central to Aihua pedagogy. Once we got started, we realised we didn't have enough teachers, and Swan sent over two more, Paddy and Cormac. These teachers all completed one year contracts, and finished at the end of the following summer. No more teachers came from Swan or contacts in Ireland after this. My contact with Ireland had dried up; in fact my contact with Ireland had never run very deep. I had to hire the next groups of teachers through Dave's ESL Cafe and thebeijinger.

Hiring foreign teachers was very hit and miss. I brought in two young ladies from Florida through Dave's ESL Cafe, who insisted that I should pay them up front for their flights. This was the only time I ever did this. We put the new teachers in the apartments that the old teachers had vacated. A couple of weeks after they arrived we waited for the

American girls and a young New Zealand guy to show up for classes. When they didn't appear, I called one of them and discovered that they were on a bus to the airport, on their way to a school in Korea. I gave our Chinese staff a speech about how we would never surrender, and then scrambled to get more teachers.

I needed teachers immediately, so I turned to thebeijigner and hired teachers already in Beijing. I encountered the strangest bunch of people. There were some lovely students among them, but they were mostly people on the run from something. I put a guilty looking guy into a classroom full of kids, and he walked out after two minutes saying he couldn't do this. I hired African guys with gleaming white button-up shirts and glasses, and the parents told me the kids were afraid the black teachers might try to eat them. I hired Philippine teachers and was told the parents only wanted caucasian teachers. I hired Russian escorts from the Bus Bar, and an excellent Irish scallywag and his Canadian girlfriend. Serbian, Dutch and French people agreed to say they were from Scotland, and we mostly got away with it.

There was an old American guy with an English or Australian accent, who sat with kids on his knee stroking their hair, even in front of parents. The Chinese staff were under instructions to never leave him alone in a classroom with students. The final straw was at a promotion in the Sculpture Park. He had the kids line up behind him and take turns kicking him in the ass, and repeating bad teacher. I had to let him go after that. To be fair though, that was the only time I had this kind of problem with a teacher.

When teachers disappeared I took over classes until I could find another teacher. Marco from Holland showed up for classes at Gu Er Xiao during a break. I was smoking and getting ready for my next class. He had never taught before, and he looked so young, like Tin Tin. I opened up his Cambridge Young Learners to a page of animals, handed it to him and said go in and say show me monkey, then do a little monkey dance. I gave him an example. I shoved him into the classroom with his book in hand and shut the door behind him. I went back to my own classroom, expecting to never see Marco again, but Marco was much tougher than he looked. He stayed at Aihua for ten years, longer than anyone except Chen Xi and me.

After many bad experiences, I put together a decent team of part time teachers to supplement the full time teachers. The part time teachers travelled out to Shijingshan from Chaoyang or Haidian. Our full time teachers would have preferred to live in Chaoyang, with the foreign restaurants, bars and discos, but I kept up a steady line about the real China, and only a few of them made midnight getaways. It was important to me to keep them housed in Shijingshan because Chaoyang was an hour away by subway, and full of bars, discos, foreign restaurants, and schools trying to hire foreign teachers.

Whenever a new group of foreign teachers arrived from abroad, we set them up in apartments and then Chen Xi would organise a beery banquet. We drank and ate and laughed. I would give a speech, and when I was drunk enough I didn't feel like a used car salesman.

We set up Zhongchu Daxia with Swan's initial investment, the 20,000 USD I'd travelled from Ireland with. There was a lot of money coming in, but there was also a lot of money going out, to foreign teachers mostly. They continued to work, grumpily at times, for 6,000 RMB per month. Chen Xi and I earned 8,000 RMB per month. Chen Xi never painted a rosy picture of our finances, or our prospects to me. At the same time the students kept coming to us in droves.

At first, Chen Xi and I were on the subway for two hours a day back and forth from Sihui Dong, but we moved back to Shijingshan not long after we opened our Zhongchudaxia centre. We took a strange two floor apartment with a roof garden, south of Babaoshan, Eight Treasures Mountain, where Beijing inters its most prestigious communist dead. Later, when Chen XI's grandmother died, I learned that it also had the industrial-strength crematorium required to serve the rest of Beijing's dead. When Chinese people asked me where I lived, I told them Babaoshan, and they always laughed at this. There were local people buried in Laoshan, to the west of Babaoshan, under little mounds of dirt, and they continued to be buried there even after these hills were transformed into the Olympic Mountain Bike course. The

Olympic velodrome hovered beside these hills like a silver UFO.

Our apartment was about a kilometre south of the Babaoshan subway station. Between our apartment and the subway there was a maze of *hutons*, the traditional style of Beijing housing, narrow lanes around one story homes that opened up on their own courtyards: *siheyuan*. To the east of these hutons was an incredible bird and flower market, which was replaced by the International Sculpture Park almost overnight in anticipation of the Olympics. Across the road from our apartment, there was a building that served as a KTV, a massage parlour, and a place for migrant workers to spend the night. There was also a slightly rough *dapaidan*. Once, someone threw coins at me from a window in the apartments above. I often sat on our rooftop among the geckos in the evenings watching screaming matches at this *dapaidan*. Some guy might stand up and start tossing plates, mugs and plastic tables at the staff or at other customers.

As at every *xiaochu* in Beijing, there was a line of illegitimate taxis waiting near the security gate. They would take you anywhere in Shijiingshan for ten RMB. These guys always tried to speak to me in Chinese, and wouldn't give up for the duration of the journey. One guy played Beijing opera, which was brutal on a hangover, and another guy played Linkin Park.

Swan sent over Paddy. He was about 40, and Oliver described him as blue blooded. He was a lovely fellow. Paddy stayed in the apartment with Chen Xi and me. He was interested in everything about China, and he loved to go into Chinese medicine shops, jade shops and other obscure boutiques at the remains of the Bird Market. He arrived home once with a gigantic, woody mushroom that was good for longevity, and he boiled this up in his teas. He bought a simple chef's hat and said his mother would love it. It was Paddy who dubbed the road running from the subway station to our apartment Dirty Street.

Paddy had a bad knee and would insist that he should sit in the front seat of the Aihua van. This annoyed me because that was my spot, and I liked to DJ from there. One night after a particularly intense session of drinking with Chen and Wang in Da Xing, Paddy sat in the front, and when I reached into the front seat between him and the driver to turn up Underworld, *Razor of Love*, he removed my hand from the dial, and turned it way down. I reached to turn it up again and he gripped me firmly by the wrist. I ripped my arm free and smashed my right fist into his face again and again. Chen Xi and the teachers pulled me back so I kicked him in the eye once and then jumped out of the van, which had pulled over to the side of the highway. Still seething, I grabbed Paddy by the hair to pull him out the window. Chen Xi jumped out and I let go of Paddy's hair and the van drove off, with Chen Xi waving it away.

It took us a good while to get a cab at the side of the highway. On the way to Shijingshan, Chen Xi calmed me down, and showed me how wrongly I had behaved. The driver had taken Paddy to her parents' apartment. We got the cab to drop us off there, and went up. Chen Xi's father answered the door and looked at me grimly, shaking his head and saying no, no, no, as though to a dog. Paddy was in the same room Chen Xi and I had stayed in when we had been married. I rapped on the door and he answered with a black eye. I apologised to him, but he didn't really accept it. Of course not. He agreed to finish the term however.

I was also having difficulties with Peter. One night at a particularly wretched *dapaidan* outside of a massage parlour on Dirty Street, perched on low stools with our knees up around our shoulders, when I stood up to emphasise my point, Peter hurled his pint glass at me. It hit me in the thigh, and left a deep, mug shaped bruise. I shaped up to fight him, but he stayed seated and Andrew pulled me aside and convinced me not to hit him. They were near the end of their year at Aihua.

Oliver and Michael were visiting to recruit students, and we met them in The Den, in Chaoyang. We were drinking beer on the plush red sofas, and Peter and Andrew were having a dispute with Swan about reimbursement for their flight. They had travelled over on business class, and Oliver was only willing to reimburse them for the price of economy. The argument became heated and Peter began insulting me. I punched him softly from across Oliver's chest, and then pulled his head down to the table by the hair. The bouncers converged on us and defused the situation with a strict warning.

Oliver and Michael met Chen Xi and me the next evening in Guomao for lemon chicken, which was all they dared to eat in China. They had brought along a guy, and they wanted to replace me with him. They suggested maybe I would be better suited to teaching. Chen Xi and I wouldn't agree to this, and they left a few days later, disappointed in Chen Xi's accountancy, and in my methods of managing people. Looking over Chen Xi's Excel sheets Michael had said to Chen Xi you're supposed to have a degree in business, and her face turned stony. We began to lose contact with Swan after this.

One Saturday morning I came in a bit late to Zhongchu Daxia, and found a mob of parents and students milling around the reception area. I was told that the police had taken the foreign teachers away. I called Chen Xi and she called Chen Fu and they were down to the school in minutes. I took the students from reception and started teaching them all together in one classroom, with desperation as my lesson plan. Chen Fu went to the police station and discovered that the Foreign Affairs police had come and taken the foreign teachers away because they were on tourist visas, and not on working visas. Chen Fu got the teachers back, and arranged for Chen Xi and me to meet the head of the Foreign Affairs Division of the Shijingshan Police that afternoon. When the teachers returned they were very upset, and it took a lot of convincing to get them back into the classrooms. They had been sitting at the police station for three hours. As I ushered them into their classrooms for the afternoon students, Yvonne kept insisting I can't go back to the police station. This is against the law. I told her Chen Xi and I were meeting the police that afternoon, and we'd sort it out, as I closed the door behind her.

Chen Xi and I met Inspector Xu, the head of Shijingshan Foreign Affairs Police, at a Korean barbecue just north of the Sculpture Park, on Chang An Jie. He was a small and exceptionally ugly man. He was already seated in the corner of the room facing the door when we arrived. As soon as we were seated, he presented me with a telescopic Chinese sword as a gift. A guy standing beside him handed it to him, and he handed it to me. The Korean owner of the restaurant served our table, and stood at attention, bowing obsequiously as he was scolded by Xu. We talked long and hard, but the meeting was fruitless. He kept coming back to the fact that we didn't have the licence to hire foreign teachers on working visas. I needed to drink *baijiu* with him, although I wasn't in the mood. When we came out of the restaurant into the late afternoon light, Chen Xi told me that he had been touching her legs under the table. She was deeply insulted and she thought he must have felt that any woman who was married to a foreign man would be more racy than a regular Chinese woman. She said that we needed Seven Uncles' help.

Seven Uncles set up another meeting with Xu the next evening. He came with us into the room Xu had occupied, but left again after only saying hello. We chatted with Xu and he told us that we would need to apply for a licence to hire foreign teachers. He said that he had a friend that might be able to help. I drank *baijiu* with Xu, and Chen Xi said we feel so small because we don't know what we can offer a man who can have anything he wants. Xu did not hesitate. He said he wanted a blonde woman. I told him I could help him realise this dream. When we left the restaurant, Xu made a show of scolding an illegal cab driver who asked us if we needed a lift. He used his mobile phone to take pictures of the poor guy, while telling him that he was chief of police, and this was not his lucky day.

Xu drove us home, and the next evening he and his driver collected me in his black Santana, and we drove into Chaoyang. We sat in the back seat and he showed me a piece of paper with 'inspector' written on it. I modelled the word a few times and then he pointed at himself and said Xu Inspector. I gathered that he was asking me to introduce him that evening as Inspector Xu. We went to Hollywood, near Ritan Park, where I knew there were Russian prostitutes. Xu's driver, whom I had not heard a word from, waited in the car. Inside Hollywood there were rough looking Russian bouncers, caucasian prostitutes, and Chinese customers. The music was pop and the lighting was dark purple. I ordered whiskey and beer for Xu and me. I ordered rounds in quick succession, and encouraged him to drink up. He had never tasted whisky before, and he seemed to enjoy it as much as I enjoyed *baijiu*. We sipped whiskey and studied the dancing women. Xu pointed out a blonde girl that he liked, and I called her over to join us at our table. I made sure that Xu heard me refer to him as Inspector Xu. The Russian lady was polite as I explained to her how important it was for me to make sure that Xu enjoyed his evening. Xu was wild-eyed and hammered, and she was dubious. I had to go higher than I'd expected to agree on a price. We went out and got into the back of Xu's Santana. Xu sat in the middle and ran his hands up and down the Russian lady, whispering obscenely. We went up to her apartment, and I waited at the kitchen table while Xu went into a room with her. There were other women in the apartment but they didn't pay any attention to me, except to give me a cup of tea. When Inspector Xu came out of the room he was strutting with his chin up and his chest out. I paid up and then led Xu down to his black Santana with the driver waiting in it. On the drive along Chang An Jie back to Shijingshan, he showed me photos on his oversized phone. The Russian lady was sitting naked on the bed, looking at her phone.

The next morning Chen Xi told me that Xu wanted to go to Hollywood again that evening, and this time he wanted two blonde girls. He collected me with his driver and Santana, and showed me the photos again as we drove back to Ritan Park. I ordered more whiskey and beer, and kept it coming. I called over a few girls, but when they saw the state of Xu they left and I had to find others. Xu was incredibly drunk and he was conducting a monologue that was full of malice, mostly in quiet whispers, but sometimes in gusts of frenzy. Some Russian bouncers came over and told me to get him out of there. Fortunately, by this time he was mostly sleeping. He was a puny guy, a little, bulbous-nosed goblin, and it was easy for me to guide and cajole him out of there. When I put him in the Santana, I got in and told the driver, *hui jia*, go home. When the driver dropped me off, Xu was snoring in a deep sleep. A few days later, Seven Uncles wanted a Russian girl. His driver waited in the black Audi as we went into Hollywood. It was much easier to find a date for Seven Uncles, with his serpentine charm. We took the girl back to Seven Uncles' office, which had a sauna and a jacuzzi. Once it was decided that she would spend the night, I was allowed to go home, and Chen Xi came in a cab to collect me.

We had a Christmas party for the foreign teachers in our apartment. I played music on my mp3 and we danced around drunk on our part of the roof, to *Protection*, by Massive Attack. I slipped out and went across to the little KTV hostel across the road. I had a beer on the red sofa in reception. I had been sneaking down here now and then for a couple of months, practising my Chinese and going into the back room with a pretty young *waidiren* with zero English. I'd learned how to say I want to serve you, in Chinese. I never asked her to take off her clothes. She would sit on the bed and I would perform my genuflexions from the corner, meekly feeding off her distance and her otherness, the exquisite whorl of her eyelid; she was a creature from the moon.

I had lost my wedding ring a few weeks before this, and I noticed now that the guy sitting beside me was wearing it. I asked him where he'd got it, and he said the other guy there, his lover, had given it to him. I pressured him to let me see it, and then I put it in my pocket and walked out of the KTV. As I left the KTV the guy I'd taken the ring from grabbed my hand and held a carpet knife to my wrist. I handed over the wedding ring. As I got out of sight, I punched into my right cheekbone several times, and blackened my eye before going back up to the Christmas party. I'd pulled this trick a couple of times in my teens, to get sympathy from girls. I told Chen XI that these guys had my wedding ring and that they had punched me up after holding the carpet knife to me. Chen Xi called Xu, and we left the party and went to the police station. When we got back everyone was gone and the party was over.

A few nights later, Xu called Chen Xi and me to a KTV, where he sat drinking *baijiu* with a beautiful *xiaojie* snuggled into either arm. He handed over my wedding ring, and told us they had brought the guy in and beaten him up, then left him dangling by one arm from a handcuff attached to a pipe in the roof until he gave up the wedding ring. He had been instructed to leave Beijing and never return. Chen Xi and I had to hang around for a while, and she had to sing a few numbers before we were able to get away.

The grand finale of our drinking bouts at Da Xing occurred just before Mr Chen was transferred to Tibet, which was a good indication that he was being groomed for a higher position in government. Chen signed a contract for us to teach his teachers for three more years. I carried Wang around on my shoulders. I took the phone number of one of the waitresses, although Wang beseeched me not to. I woke up with chunks torn out of my memory. I was in my bed, and my legs were completely black and blue. I looked at them in astonishment, and found bruises everywhere, deep and purple, bruises on top of bruises. I remembered getting out of the van at the nearby supermarket. I remembered Chen Xi shouting at me and hitting me. A girl who worked in the shop where the van had stopped later told me that Chen Xi punched me, and I fell flat on my back on the sidewalk.

Laying there in bed I pieced it together. Chen Xi had left me at the side of the road, and asked two guys I had hired locally a week before to get me up to our apartment, where they were staying with us. Chen Xi had gone with the bus back to her parents' house. These two guys, wall eye from Liverpool, and a big sleepy doofus from Toronto, both in Beijing on the off-chance of finding work as teachers, dragged me up to the apartment, and that was where all the bruises must have come from. I needed them to keep teaching for a while, so I said nothing about the bruises, and even found them an apartment near ours. I kept them teaching for as long as I could, until they pulled the inevitable midnight get-away right after getting paid.

Paul Gentle was from Alabama. He had a PhD in Economics. At the interview he told me that he loved Chinese students because they were so polite. If you fell asleep in the class, when you woke they would just be sitting there quietly, waiting for the class to proceed. I paused with a smile, waiting for him to laugh, before realising this was not intended to be funny. I hired him on the spot, and as part of the deal, he moved into the apartment with Chen Xi and me that afternoon.

A few days after Paul arrived, the lady who cleaned our apartment, Huang Ayi, called Chen Xi and told her that Paul was screaming at her, but she didn't understand what the problem was. Chen Xi and I got a cab to the apartment. Paul was wild-eyed as he told me he couldn't find his medication. We spoke to Huang Ayi and she showed us where she had put away some bottles of pills. I jotted down the names of the medicines before I gave them back to Paul. I Yahoo'd this later and found it was medicine for severe bipolar disorder.

Paul would wake up each morning in an absolute mess, hardly able to speak. I found that if I spoke to him about American history, it would awaken him and get him chuckling. I would walk him to the top of Dirty Street to join the other teachers on the school bus to Da Xing. He would complain about the rudeness of the Chinese, and whenever a car cut him off he would slap the roof and roar at the driver.

It was always with a sigh of relief that I slid shut the door of the school van behind him.

Da Xing complained that he would often shout at the students, who were adults and teachers, and that once he just walked out of the classroom and spent the rest of the morning sitting where the school bus was due to collect them. Once he'd taken out a newspaper and sat reading it ostentatiously at the front to the class. I gave Paul pep talks, and talked him through the teaching material. Da Xing was willing to accept my line that Paul was a troubled genius, considering that some of the other teachers were doing so well. Paul confided in me of his own accord that he had bipolar disorder. He told me that once he thought he had contact lenses in when he didn't, and damaged his eyes trying to get them out. He told me about people he'd had trouble with in the past, and how they'd written emails to him on made up e-mail accounts using other people's names. They had also sent emails to other people in his name.

At this time I hired the giant Daniel, who was also from Alabama. In the interview he told me that he was in China to avoid paying alimony. We put him in an apartment with his Chinese girlfriend. At our start of term party, he and Paul sang *I Wish I was in DIxie*. I was drunk, and I made the mistake of telling Daniel that although he was very big I could beat him in a fight.

After a couple of weeks, Daniel was not happy with his wages, he felt that he could earn more teaching privately. He came in just before his classes on Saturday, and demanded that I pay him then and there for the work he'd done so far. I got a teacher who was meant to be on a break to jump into his class, and told Daniel that as soon as he was out of the apartment I would pay him. He came back later in the afternoon, and I agreed to go with him to see that the apartment was left in a reasonable state, and pay him after I had the key. Daniel's girlfriend had brought her brother in his armoured car, along with his security team. We sat in the back with a few little guys in uniforms and helmets.

When we got to the apartment block in Pingguoyuar, we went up to the apartment. The security guys from the armoured car came up also. I looked around the apartment, and pointed out that some things were not as tidy as they should be. His girlfriend was incensed by this, and after she whispered to him, he took off his jacket, pulled up his sleeves and said he gits beat now. This guy was way too big for me. I stood by the window wondering if I could escape that way, and then I went down the stairs when he moved away from the door. I anticipated an attack as he clattered down the stairs behind me.

When I got outside, I called Chen Xi while he stalked me, demanding his money. I asked Chen Xi to send the police. He stalked me around the common ground in front of the building, bellowing gimme ma gawd damn money! Local people gathered and watched the spectacle. The security guards were hanging out at the armoured car with their electric batons. Chen Fu showed up in the school van, with a convoy of cars behind him. Seven Uncles and other members of the family got out of the cars in tweed blazers and stood around me. Daniel felt that this meant it was time to fight and he squared up to me, making a great show of putting up his dukes. I went to Chen Fu and told him to give me the money, but he looked at me with scorn and said no.

Chen Fu got out of the school van stiffly, went over to the girlfriend and demanded the key. There seemed to be no messing with grouchy old Chen Fu. The girlfriend handed over the key, then Chen Fu gave me the money for Daniel, locking my eyes in a world-weary gaze. I kept my distance from Daniel as I handed him the cash.

A few days later, Inspector Xu and a team of police came to Zhongchu Daxia, and I told them about Daniel as they sat on the sofa. They told me that to run this school I would need to manage the teachers on my own. Out of curiosity, one of the police asked to see a photo of Daniel. The only one we had was of him standing beside me at one of the primary school promotions. The police chuckled as they passed the photo around. At 200 pounds I was a big man, but Daniel was easily 280.

I managed to get a few new guys in and get rid of Paul. He had fallen in love with our bookkeeper, Cathy, but when he asked her to marry him she turned him down. When he stormed into the office at Zhongchu Daxia, accusing me of having advised Cathy against marrying him, I told him that he couldn't work at Aihua anymore. Over the coming months, he sent me emails in other teacher's names, from made up email accounts, accusing me of drug-use and prostitution. He once phoned me from Daniel's phone to tell me Daniel was coming around to kick the shit out of me. I kept looking over my shoulder going up and down Dirty Street for the next few weeks.

THE BEIJING UNDERGROUND

I found a little gym at Shijingshan Tiyuguan, the local sports stadium, where you could pay as you went. I was in the gym doing some weights when I heard the sound of a heavy bag being kicked with great power. I went through the door to the gymnasium. There were mats spread at the far end, and several heavy bags hanging from an iron bar. About twenty young Chinese guys were practising kicks and throws. The gym attendant tried to stop me from going down, but I went down anyway, pretending I couldn't understand what she was saying. The young guys were all bald. They didn't stop what they were doing but watched me as I walked over to the bags.

I grabbed a pair of bag gloves. They were wet inside. The gym attendant apologised to the trainer. I tuned everything out and started to hit the bag. Hitting the bag had been my thing since I was seventeen years old, and I was good at it. I got my own bag mitts and began to come down to hit the bag every morning.

The young guys training in the gym were Shaolin novitiates. They were vegetarian, and wouldn't drink. They trained every morning, every afternoon, and every evening. They all lived together in one room off the gym and ate rice porridge in the morning from tin bowls. They had zero English so I tried to speak to them in Chinese. We could only talk about the most basic things: have you eaten? was it tasty? it is raining, or the weather is good. Their trainer, Chen Shifu, led the Shaolin monks when they travelled abroad to perform.

I offered to buy a bag for the gym so that I wouldn't have to push past the gym attendant every day. I gave Chen Shifu 1000 RMB, and he got a huge leather bag of about 200 kg.

This bag was a pleasure to hit. I had a CD player that I listened to while I hit the bag. I loved the rhythm, the stiff snap of a jab, the thunder of a combination, the feet beneath sending everything up through the toes. I listened to Tristania, *World of Glass*. Its anger and rage pushed me through walls of exhaustion. *Go Away*, *Give* and *The Switch* by Cold, that growl, the Power that was channelled through me. With all the movement involved in hitting the bag, the CD player often skipped, and I welcomed the advent of MP3 players. My training regime was so different from that of the Shaolin novitiates. For them it was discipline and skill, and for me it was rage and endurance.

Some time after I started hitting the bag in the Tiyuguan, one of our past teachers, Breda Lee, who had done her PhD in Cork on the topic of the Uighur minority in China, sent me an email telling me that beneath the Shijignshan Tiyuguan there was an underground prison, and she asked me if I ever saw Uighurs being taken in. Uighurs were easy to recognise, because they looked different from Han Chinese, and they wore a particular type of pillbox cap. After she mentioned this, I did notice white buses with Uighurs in them, being driven into the stadium. I imagined this underground prison as somewhere linked to the fabled underground city of Beijing, built as bunkers during the cold war. Some years later I drove past the Tiyuguan at four in the morning and saw a body beneath the underpass. A blue truck was pulled over to the side of the road. The body's thighs were torn up like hamburger, but I noticed there was no blood. I wondered if this was because the body was already dead when it was hit by the truck. Were these shredded thighs a blip from the underground city of pain beneath the stadium?

We had made no progress in getting licensing to hire foreign teachers, and Xu continued to put the squeeze on us. He told us that his contacts in the Beijing Foreign Affairs Bureau were busy now, but would get around to us soon. One day the building manager of Zhongchudaxia introduced us to John Liu, the government leader of Shijingshan District. John was an intelligent and friendly guy, who had studied for a year at Harvard, and was doing a PhD in Tsinghua. He invited Chen Xi and me to dinner at Hualian Garden Hotel. As we were ushered in by a team of staff, he told us that this was his building. He often told us that buildings were his, if they were owned by the local government. He was not a vain person though, and he was very easy to get along with.

We began to meet John regularly for meals. John liked to eat like a Roman Senator; his palate did not observe foreign niceties. He gave me a vat of *baijiou* with seahorses floating in it, and Chen Xi told me that this was good for man-power. His daughter, Ting Ting, would sit on his lap tugging at his prosperous earlobes. He never drank, but he liked to see me drink. I started teaching an adult class, and it filled up very quickly once people knew that John was attending.

About a month after we met John, Chen Xi and I had a meeting with two guys from Beijing Foreign Affairs at a famous dim sum restaurant kitty-corner from the Lama Temple, Jing Ding Xie. Within a month, we had all of the licences we needed to hire foreign teachers with Z-visas. A couple of years after we met him, John was promoted from leader of Shijingshan District to head of Beijing Police and Security. He continued to protect Chen Xi and me until Xi Jing Ping began his crackdown on corruption toward the final years of our time in Beijing.

Xu was fired as the head of Shijingshan Foreign Affairs Police when he fell asleep at the wheel, ploughed into a parked car, and remained sleeping, stinking of *baijiu*, until other police gathered at the scene the next morning. The next head of Shijingshan Foreign Affairs Police was a much more respectable person. He visited us and we arranged for me to go to the police station daily to give English classes to the local Foreign Affairs police. I played *High Voltage* by Lincoln Park, and asked them to try and write down the words. I gave them a DVD of *Bloody Sunday*, and asked them to watch it. We did a lot of role-plays, and I made up scenarios in which foreigners were misbehaving in Beijing. I pretended to be a Texan with a bottle of whiskey sitting up on the shoulders of the statue of Mao at Junshi Bowuguan, the Military Museum, and they coaxed me down politely. I met Da Gao at this class, and he was our go-to person in the local police from this time forward. He was distant, quiet, polite and highly moral. I was never able to tempt him to a beer. He kept an eye on me, and always knew what mischief I was getting up to. I think he considered me to be an exotic animal.

Grace Pan, our Foreign Affairs Officer, would meet with me in an empty classroom to discuss foreign teacher applications. She wore a short skirt and sat on the sofa across from me, crossing and uncrossing her legs. She let a high-heeled shoe dangle from her foot. I asked about her boyfriend, and she told me he was too German for her, too sensible. She said she wanted passion and crazy laughter in her life. She asked me about my book on Joyce, and I told her all about it. I explained to her that I dreamed of being a chaste slave to a woman who was untouchable and ideal.

Grace played along as I weaved this fantasy around her, and I soon became obsessed.

I was active on the *That's Beijing* personals, and *Adult Friendfinder*. I introduced Grace to a German guy I'd met online. Dirk was about 6'7. He played enigma while they kissed on his sofa and he rubbed his hands over her clothed body, and then up under her skirt. I sat in his armchair watching quietly, listening to Grace's sighs.

Another time I took her to a Chinese dominatrix with a German husband. They lived in a plush apartment across from Suzy Wong's at the East Gate of Chaoyang Park. She and Grace sat on the sofa, and the dominatrix ordered me to crawl around the coffee table naked in front of them before whipping me against the door. Grace began to suggest that I had this great dream of not being able to have sex with her because I was unable to perform. When I told her that wasn't true, she asked me to prove it.

Chen Xi and I had not been getting on. We would struggle with Aihua all day in Zhongchu Daxia, and then talk about Aihua problems over dinners, through the evening and into bed. She and I were opposite. She was strict and efficient at work, while I was jolly and charming. When I called her Chen Xi at school, she would hiss, Ms Chen. I took to calling her Ms Chen at all hours. I often criticised her for being too strict with the Chinese staff.

I was asked to deliver a series of ten lectures at Tsinghua University, on the topic of the History of Western Thought. There were a few hundred people in the lecture hall as I opened my blue and yellow PPT, and started in on Aristotle and Plato. By the time we got to the last lecture, there were ten people, and we made a circle of chairs on the stage to talk about Joyce. I was given an envelope full of pink 100 RMB notes at the dinner after the last lecture.

Grace accompanied me to the lectures at Tsinghua in her capacity as Foreign Affairs Officer of Aihua. I felt horrible the first day I went to her apartment. I knew that I was crossing a Rubicon. Betrayal clung like grit to the city. I was aware that I didn't want to do this, but I felt compelled to get into a cab with her outside of Zhongchu Daxia.

In my heart, I knew that even if it was only this once, or twice, if I went now it meant the end of my marriage, the end of my limited domestic integrity. I felt so mean, so small, so ignoble. But Grace was willing to let me live out my erotic fantasy, and I felt I owed it to myself to explore this compulsion, in order to be most true to myself. I knew Chen Xi could never help me learn what was at the bottom of it all. I risked losing everything, but by the time I got in the cab, I had convinced myself that Chen Xi was my ally, and that she would understand why I needed to do this. I summoned Blake to to appease my regrets.

Grace lived near Seven Uncles in the depths of Pingguoyuar. I was so noticeable. The next time I visited her apartment I had obtained knock-off viagra from a little street-side sex shop, where the salesman dressed like a pharmacist. I had to ask for it by making a gesture with my forearm and fist.

My first lockdown was SARS. Suddenly classes were stopped, and teachers returned to their home countries. I went to the Irish Embassy and got visas for Chen Xi and Grace. It seemed important for them to get out of Beijing. I would stay on my own on Dirty Street. Chen Xi flew first for Dublin. Grace travelled to Dublin a week later, and she spent that week with me in the apartment I shared with Chen Xi. Grace had decided to resign from Aihua, and this was to be our grand finale.

After Grace left for Dublin, lockdown proper began. I stood at the window looking out at the empty KTV. There was no *dapaindan*. The people I saw moved furtively, in masks. I overheard dreadful domestic battles, with broken glass and shrieking. I wrote the history of my sexual perversity, right up to my vision of the Goddess of Infinite Mercy, Mongolian girls gathered round me, and sent it in a group email to all the people in my contacts.

None of this was by choice. I did not control my sexual compulsion. It would pick a tangent and drive me in this direction through a ceaseless subliminal whispering that became a roaring when I was aroused. I bent to its will to accommodate, thinking that since it was tied to me I may as well seek some compromise. It dug its claws into every part of me.

From the beginning this hunger for self abasement was inextricably tied up with my sexuality. The more I held it back the fiercer it grew. It drove me to put myself in many degrading and dangerous situations.

I received an email back from a Joyce scholar, Richard Stack, snidely describing the rapture of my eroticism as after the style of Gerty McDowell. When I received no other feedback, I sent more group emails, berating them all as representatives of the human race. Peter, my Uncle in Botswana, replied: same to you, wanker. He'd hit the nail on the head. A few years later he died of prostate cancer without even telling my dad he was sick.

After a month of lockdown alone in the apartment, I could bear no more, and I walked down Dirty Street to Babaoshan *ditie,* and got on the underground for Chaoyang. There were only a couple of people in each car and they were in masks. I went first to Maggie's. There was only an obese, bald guy and three Mongolian girls hanging round his rack of luminous, test-tube shots. I left without getting a drink, and walked past Frank's Place. Through the window I saw everyone lift up together, arms in the air. Someone on the TV must have scored. I went down toward the Den, where there would also be sports on TV, but maybe a few Mongolian girls hovering round. As I approached the Den, I heard *Emancipate yourself from mental slavery,* and I caught the pungent odour of pot. I looked into a fenced-off area to the left and saw a bunch of black guys in plastic chairs smoking joints in front of a bus. It was the Bus Bar. I went in and sat at their table. They lifted their hands to shake mine. They tried to do a snapping thing with our middle fingers as we broke the grip. They said, s'up dog, and passed me a joint. I sat down and ordered a beer.

They were Nigerians, and I became buddies with them: Ben, Larry, Andie, Silva and Jude. We were all outsiders here. I managed to score a little baggie of weed before I left, and I used this to write poetry when I got home. The History of my Sexual Perversity had been yet another utter failure, I realised now, and I was working on skinny, unrhyming sonnets, attempting to snatch moments from oblivion, to stop all these seconds from continuing to disappear into days gone by.

Every couple of days I would go into the Bus Bar to drink and smoke with the Nigerians. Once I met some of them in another place, a cramped loft where Tupac blared and I sat in the dark corner sending around reefer after reefer of sticky black hash and drinking whiskey, among floating eyes and alien flesh.

After getting wasted with the Nigerians, I would go snooping around Sanlitun solo. That's how I discovered The Club. With the Olympics coming, Sanlitun, the pub and nightclub district of Chaoyang, felt like it could actually house an alternative culture. Henry Ng was the owner of the Club. Quentin Tarantino hung out here when he was filming

Kill Bill. They played progressive house, mixing in snatches from Nirvana, and there were a lot of drugs.

I would stay dancing in the small, discrete mob until the early hours. Once I went into a back room and sat on a red sofa at a table with a couple of Chinese guys and their girls. One of the Chinese guys put a huge line of something on the table, and offered me a rolled up 100 RMB note. I understood one of the Chinese girls asking him if I knew what it was. I snorted up the whole line, and went back to the dance floor. The music was majestic, crashing waves, smashing at my feet, cascading down fast from the miles above me. My scalp was crawling with sweat and my hair stood up on end. I began to unravel. I lurched to the toilets, and crawled into a cubicle, pressing open the door with one arm. The walls of the cubicle became green moss and I sunk my fingers in. My head became a stone then, in the shape of my head but with no human detail, and I held it up in my hands so that it wouldn't sink into the sea of moss all around me. Across the sea clouds were broken open in heaven's ladders beneath a laughing golden Buddha looking down at me laughing at me holding up the stone that was my head way up into the crashing open yellow crayon alleluia light.

When I went back out to the dance floor I saw Benito, a top French party animal, standing against a pillar pressing his hands to his face. I helped him to the toilets and left him there to his visions. When he came out we drank whiskey and smoked joints into the wee hours. He told me the guy who'd given us the lines was the son of a general, and that we had taken something designed by the Chinese military, but I thought it was probably ketamine.

After SARS was over, and Chen Xi returned from Dublin, she discovered Grace's scrunchy in our shower. She demanded that I shouldn't lie to her, and so I said nothing. A few weeks later we moved to Jie Shi Ping, a new development on Chang An Jie next to Hualian Garden Hotel, because she couldn't bear to sleep in the bed that Grace had been in, or have a shower where she'd discovered Grace's scrunchy.

Beijing was changing quickly. They broadened Dirty Street into a respectable thoroughfare that ran under the Second Ring Road into Fengtai. The hutongs north of our old place became a community of twenty grey and yellow tower blocks: Yuan Yang Shan Shui. They built Pullman's, and the Wanda Plaza. I visited Grace a few times up in the distant, northwest corner of Beijing. She phoned a few times and insisted that I cut all ties with Chen Xi and Aihua. I couldn't even consider this. I knew that I would never give up Aihua, and that my life was tied to Chen Xi's. Grace mocked the words of devotion I had given her.

When *Joyce and the Perverse Ideal* was published, I received four copies in the mail. When I showed it to Chen Xi we had a fight because on the acknowledgements page beneath her own name there was reference to my dear friend, Grace Pan. I was ashamed, and I donated three of my books to ladies at the Mongolian Embassy, the ones who had together become the Goddess of Infinite Mercy. They made no show of wanting to receive these books, but I pressed them on them. When I got around to telling Grace that I couldn't leave Chen Xi, she married the German Chef from Swiss Otel, and I never heard from her again. A few weeks later Chen Xi told me to fuck off over the phone when she was out with friends one evening. She got a short haircut to spite me and then moved out. I still saw her at work every day as we continued to manage Aihua together.

Chen Xi and I attended a big dinner with her family, and I handed Seven Uncles a powerful reefer of sticky black hash. I'd packed it especially full because on a first try people sometimes feel nothing. He passed out, and was taken to the toilet to vomit.

AIHUA CLASSIC

Toward the end of Spring 2005, we moved from our centre at Zhongchudaxia, to an independent school house attached to Gu Liu Primary school. We were not actually allowed to rent from the public school system, just as we were not actually allowed to send foreign teachers into public schools, but regulations in Shijingshan were slack, and with the Olympics coming we were allowed to do many things that we weren't supposed to do. Foreigners in general were able to get away with almost anything, and young foreigners were running rampant in Chaoyang and Haidian. At this time, the police did not want to be involved in anything to do with foreigners. They were often too shy to want to use English, and there was a lot of paperwork involved.

Most of the foreigners coming to China were young people reinventing themselves. It was the time and place of the Fake Celebrity. Foreign women didn't usually date Chinese guys, so that the men coming to China were of interest to the foreign women as well as Chinese. The young white guys were punching way above their weight when it came to dating Chinese women. Chinese men hated when Chinese women dated foreign guys, but the resentment didn't really make itself apparent until after the Olympics, when you had reports of Chinese guys driving around Sanlitun with bats and bars in their cars, looking to pummel some smug, outlandish white Lothario.

There was excitement about the coming Beijing Olympics. The local people all wanted their kids to learn English, and interact with foreign people. For foreigners, Beijing was a cool place to be. So many foreign people, just out of college, or lost for direction, wanted to experience Beijing. We were nicely caught in the middle of these two populations.

When we first looked at the building attached to Guliu Xiao, it was a mess, and I was against the move. There were migrant workers sleeping in it, and it was full of dust, debris, tea jars and empty tubs of instant noodles. Chen Fu found this place for us through his connections with the Education Bureau. The rent was much lower than at Zhongchu Daxia, and it was more suited to our purpose. It was an independent school house of three stories, with a small courtyard out front. Gu Liu Primary School was our landlord, and our relations were good at first.

Gu Liu Primary School and the rubberised sports pitch that separated our buildings was to the south. I stood at the window watching the primary-school kids doing callisthenics to the commands of the headmaster over a PA system cranked up to full volume, or sometimes goose-stepping in red scarves and military uniforms, cradling fake automatic rifles.

We were deeper now in Shijignshan, in a dense maze of *xiaochu*. There were blue and yellow iron exercise stations for old people. The old guys stood on one leg and rubbed their calves against horizontal bars. I would always try to have a chat with them.

I was engaged in frequent battles with people parking in front of our gates. There were more and more cars in Beijing, and by the time I had a car, it was almost impossible to find a place to park. Sometimes Chen Xi or I had to send out Sam or Fan Cheng to drive our cars around until they found a spot.

Attached to the front of the building was a row of shacks. The first of these was a little shop where I bought sachets of Nescafe 2+1, cigarettes, a tarry black egg, or a tin of beer. I practised my Chinese with the shopkeepers, an old couple who slept in one of the aisles, discussing in very general terms how our respective days were going. Once our classes opened this little shop made a roaring trade, so my relationship with these people was good. In the other shacks pressed against the front of our building, there was something that sometimes seemed to be a garage, a tiny restaurant in which the proprietors also slept, and a window from behind the curtain of which a dour, middle aged face sometimes blinked.

We faced a six story housing block to the north. On two occasions someone jumped from the roof of this building. There was a fight over a little dog a driver had hit without remorse. The young driver punched the old guy who owned the dog. He fell down and hit his head on the pavement and died on the spot. There were grannies with red armbands in charge of public morale. They sat on brick walls chatting, watching. To the north was the gated entryway onto Changanjie. There were *bao an* here, and at the entry to the school. Red banners communicating current government sentiment were hung from the walking bridge over Changanjie: *order for together prosperity.*

Changanjie was blocked to pedestrians but you could go north to Gucheng Lu across the walking bridge, where people sold DVDs and nicknacks, or down through the underground station. From the bridge you looked west to the gates of Shougang Iron and Steel.

You entered the courtyard of our school house through black, cast-iron gates, with a door sized opening in the centre. Our courtyard was carpeted with astroturf that soon became yellow with dust. This wall of the school was covered in orange marble tiles with our name in golden Chinese characters. To brighten the city up for the Olympics, the local government painted the rest of the outside of our building orange. Beside the door into the school, there was a billboard with my smugly grinning head floating in a cloud beside 'Aihua' in exploding Chinese characters. A little flight of concrete steps lead up to a secure iron door painted navy blue. There was an ornate lamp of a European style and a security camera above the door. At the start of classes on weekends and evenings, I would be at the top of the steps leading into the school, welcoming the parents, and bantering with the kids. I had Fan Cheng set up the first 20 seconds of *Love Generation*, by Bob Sinclair, as our school bell, and at the start of every class this played from the speaker above the door, and in all the halls and classrooms.

On entering the school house you faced a hallway running the length of the school, with a line of windows facing north onto the backs of the shacks in front of the school. The doors to the rooms ran along the south of this corridor. There were security cameras and water coolers in the corridors and in all of the rooms. The walls were white and there were slogans along the roof-beams across the corridor. During classes we would put out stools for the parents in the corridors, and they would sit or stand around the doors, listening in on their kid's classes. I would stop to talk to them, and they were very gracious in their praise of our teachers and our school.

Parents would bring their kids in to inquire about classes, and our sales people, who worked on commission, would try to sell our onsite classes. A foreign teacher might be called in by a salesperson to do a placement test for a kid, which usually closed the deal, but if it didn't, the salespeople might allow the parents to watch on-going classes on the security cameras.

At the end of the first floor corridor was the Admin Office, behind a secure iron door. Li Miao was in charge of this office. She was Chen Xi's Personal Assistant. She was one of those Chinese people who cannot recognise that foreign people are fully human, and over the years I had many disputes with her. Fan Cheng was in charge of IT and the security system. The security camera played on his computer, and sometimes I would sit with him and spy on people in other rooms. Sam was the driver, and when not driving he would sit playing games on his phone. Li Miao, Fan Cheng and Sam were local Shijingshan people and they stayed at Aihua longer than anyone else. As far as I know they are still with AIhua. They had no interest in learning English, and I learned most of my Chinese from Sam and Fan Cheng. Accountants changed frequently, usually because of the pressure they received from Chen Xi.

The Teaching Department's Administrative Office was lorded over by the tall and regal Madame Wang, a retired local headmaster that we took on at the bequest of the Education Committee. She was in charge of the commission system for the Chinese staff. We appointed a Chinese teacher as a coordinator of each of the public schools that we sent teachers into, and they all reported to Madam Wang. She acted as a matron to the young Chinese teachers, resolving disputes and encouraging positive attitudes. She was big-hearted, and open-minded. She had no English, and she was always apologising to me for this.

The Foreign Affairs Officer was in charge of visa applications for foreign teachers, registering new teachers with the police, collecting new teachers at the airport, and delivering them to their Shijingshan accommodation. She was also in charge of processing foreign teacher wages.

From the windows of our largest classroom at the end of the second floor corridor I would sometimes watch the kids from Guliu in the rubberised pitch between our building and theirs, standing in long ranks, listening to shrill speeches from their school leaders, or doing callisthenics. When the ones in the back row caught sight of me leaning out the window with my cigarette and Nescafe 2+1, they would point me out to one another and call out hello. When the public school teachers patrolling the ranks noticed this they would berate and sometimes batter the kids back into place, without looking up at me.

Most of the third floor was occupied by the Records Department of the Shijingshan Education Bureau. We had two rooms to the west of the stairwell, containing grumpy old Chen Fu, our Assistant Headmaster in charge of PR, and

Wang Hui, our Marketing Manager. She was forty, on surface fat and jolly, but also cunning, small hearted and manipulative. She was considered Chen Xi's right hand and spy. She came in for a lot of abuse from Chen Xi and Chen Fu, but she could stick it. She had no English, so our communication was always superficial, and my ideas, expressed in Chinese, seemed infantile to her.

I couldn't get on with the young lads in marketing. They had some English, but they would insist on speaking to me in Chinese, to put me at a disadvantage. Whenever I asked them to do something they would tell me that they needed to check with Chen Xi first. No matter how much I insisted that our school colours were navy, white, silver and a touch of orange, all of our billboards and fliers wound up with red backgrounds and yellow characters.

At the western end of the third floor hall was Chen Xi's office. I didn't have an office or even a desk for the first couple of years. I would just find a spot somewhere. Eventually I was given a big desk pressed against Chen Xi's, my own computer and a spinny executive chair.

The atmosphere in this office was tense. I often left the room with mugs shattering on the wall beside my head. Despite our terrible arguments, and the abusive way that she dealt with the long line of penitents coming in to report to her each day, I felt compassion for Chen Xi, and I knew that as far as her treatment of me was concerned, I was getting what I deserved. As for the others, the people in the departments that she worked with were factional, manipulative and lazy, and I didn't often feel sorry for them. I might tell Chen Xi that I was trying to protect her, not them, by urging her to remain calmer, and not get so angry, but no argument could change her ways. We were both under so much pressure keeping up our own sides of the show.

When I walked through the school I could laugh and joke with parents, students and staff. Chen Xi slipped in and out of the office furtively. While parents treated me as an honoured guest, they saw her as a local opportunist with a high opinion of herself. I was natural and at ease with children, but when Chen Xi had to stop and talk to a kid, it was awkward.

Although Chen Xi was strict with the staff, she was respected and well liked by people in the Teaching Department. She was the one who organised the banquets. The Chinese staff knew that all of the legal liability for the school was on her head. If one of our thousands of kids broke a leg or a finger on our premises, Chen Xi would need to answer for it.

Sam spent his days shuttling teachers to and from our offsite teaching locations. They would joke and laugh with Sam, who drove like a demon to even get out of the *xiaochu* and onto Changanjie. He honked away at any possible impingement on his passage, and the teachers engaged in a jovial running commentary on the bizarre world in which they were immersed.

Sam's shuttling of teachers was endless. We were taking on more and more off site programs. We were doing corporate training for Shougang. We were teaching old people, police, factory workers and soldiers. We were even teaching the ambassador of Kazakhstan. We taught at four Shijingshan kindergartens in the mornings. In the afternoons we were sending teachers into four primary schools, and two high schools.

One of these schools was Jingyuan, the most prestigious school in Shijingshan, and the kids here were the naughtiest. Students at other schools could be high spirited but were never cheeky. The kids at Jingyuan were smart asses, and they saw our classes as a chance to blow off steam. They also had the best English.

Most of our on-site students were from Jingyuan. The parents of Jingyuan students had more money, a bit of English, and were not afraid to express themselves.

It was hard to keep teachers working at Jingyaun Xiuxiao. Some would come back to the school after classes at Jingyuan and break down crying in the teachers lounge. Part-time teachers would just disappear, and full-time teachers renegotiating their contracts would stipulate that they would not be sent into Jingyuan. Depending on the quality of the teacher, I would do my best to uphold my end of this agreement.

In the summer of 2006, John Liu took Chen Xi and me to meet the Headmistress of Wu Yi Xiuxiao, where Ting Ting was a student. Over a beautiful meal in a stunning venue, we agreed to open classes at her school. This was our biggest project yet, and we would be teaching twelve classes simultaneously, three afternoons a week. We hired another bus and driver. Wu Yi was just outside of Shijingshan, in Haidian, but only a half kilometre south of Yonganli subway station, so part time teachers coming to teach from Chaoyang or Haidian could walk here from the subway station.

Zhongchu Daxia had been converted offices, but now we really had a school. We completed renovations a few days before the start of our summer classes. On the first day, though, the parents congregated in a mob in the courtyard. The parents didn't want to send their kids into our new school because of the smell of paint. I debated long and hard with the ringleader, who was very proud of his English, but eventually we had to agree to finish summer classes in Zhongchu Daxia. Chen Xi and Chen Fu had stony faces over this, because it wasn't easy for them to negotiate more time in Zhongchu Daxia, and because it was an extra expense we didn't need. I began to understand why there were stab vests and electric batons at the security gates of all the schools.

I experienced my most severe parent mob one Christmas. We had brought in hundreds of kids who were not enrolled at Aihua for an elaborate Christmas party, where they changed rooms to meet different teachers for different

Christmas activities. When it was over, the parents, migrant workers who could not afford to send their kids to Aihua, were at the school gates, waiting for their kids. The foreign teachers had slipped off. The senior Chinese management disappeared and Ivy Huang and I let the children through our gates one by one, into the hands of a parent.

It was snowing. Parents who saw their kids waiting shoved to the front and called to them to come out the gates, but we kept the kids in place so that we would not have a crush of people at the door we'd opened in the centre of the gates. I shut the door on the parents and told the seething mob to make space for the kids to get out. One very angry guy kept calling me *laowai*. Things were hairy, but I established order and got the kids out. As we got the last kids out, Da Geng, our liaison with the local Police, showed up and scolded me for half an hour while we waited on Chen Xi to arrive from dinner somewhere to receive her half hour of scolding.

It was perhaps a good thing that we didn't run summer classes at our Gucheng Center in 2005, as this gave us the summer to assemble and train a Chinese team to work with the new foreign teachers arriving late August, for the start of the next school year. By the end of that summer, we had thirty Chinese members of staff trained and ready to go. The Admin, Sales and Marketing people didn't speak English, and I was not usually involved in the interviews or the training process. They were subject to Chinese management. The bulk of the new hires though were Chinese teachers, who worked in the tense tug of war between Chinese Management and me as Academic Director, in charge of the Teaching Department.

Despite the cost, we had decided to put a Chinese co-teacher into every class. Chen Xi and I interviewed co-teachers through June and July until we had the required number. Most of the Chinese teachers were young women from outside Beijing, who had recently graduated from their hometown colleges. Their English levels varied wildly, and we encountered the most peculiar accents. Most of them seemed childlike and naive on the surface. There were so many hello kitty pencil cases and binders.

The foreign teachers had no had no idea how squalid and poor were the backgrounds of most of these Chinese teachers. We rented apartments for the Chinese teachers and put them in dormitories of eight to a room. They were at first nervous around the foreign teachers, but would quickly gain more confidence. A few of the best were married local ladies who had just called in from the street looking for work. The discount for their kids to study at Aihua was their main incentive. They provided some stability and maturity to the teaching team.

Once we had all staff hired, we put them in red t-shirts with our logo at the breast and provided them with training on school culture. Chen Fu and Chen Xi spent their time developing increasingly intricate bonus systems and pay grades based on renewal rates. Chen Fu wrote a test for the new staff, based on our promotional material. A lot of the questions were about my many distorted achievements.

By the end of the summer we had the Chinese staff ready for the arrival of the next batch of foreign teachers. When we called them all together in the school courtyard it was astonishing to see the size of the team of red shirts. We sent them out through the local communities with red flyers and banners. Leaders carried clipboards.

After Jackie Yao left, Chen Xi and I interviewed people to replace him. We were very lucky to find Lilly as our Chinese Teacher Trainer. She had experience working in kindergartens. In the interview she was bubbly and hilarious as she immediately started teaching us English as though we were small children.

We learned from Lilly how to teach through play. Many of the Chinese teachers adopted Lily's mannerisms, and her laughter echoed through the school. Lily was great with kids, but took a lot of abuse for her lack of administrative skills from Chen Xi and Chen Fu, and left because of this.

We replaced Lily with one of the Chinese teachers that we had at hand. Ivy Huang was stricter and more mature, which we kind of needed then. Our classes were fun, but they were chaotic, and there was no real way of evaluating learning. Ivy added discipline and method to the madness of our classes. She structured the Chinese teaching team into Officers and Managers of this function and that. She was more thick-skinned than Lily, and she stayed with us until 2013, when her husband, Ray Murphy, our second foreign teacher trainer, took Ivy with him to live in Dublin.

When the September 2005 foreign teachers arrived we had everything in place. Finlay Beaton, with his Sean Connery accent and goatee, had been teaching in Russia, and then with EF in northeast China. He became Director of Studies; I negotiated the responsibilities, while Chen Xi negotiated payment. She was very conscious of costs, and drove a hard bargain.

Finlay acted as a buffer between the foreign teachers and me. They were to come to him when they had a problem, and he would take them to a nearby restaurant to discuss this over beer and *yangrouchuan'r*. I attempted to hover over the whole thing, only touching it when necessary.

When Finlay left, Ray took over the role. Ray was dating Ivy, the Chinese Teacher Trainer, and they coordinated our system. Ray was less personable than Finlay, but he was more meticulous and systematic. In retrospect it seems much of Aihua's success was down to Ivy and Ray, and after they left the venture began to seem hollow.

When we opened our new Gucheng Center in September 2005 we had twelve foreign teachers. By 2015 we had fifty. I mostly hired teachers from ESL Cafe, but I got help from David Cooney, a Dublin guy who ran Teachers for Asia.

Our full time foreign teachers were mostly in their mid to late twenties, and recently graduated. When they arrived, Sam and the Foreign Affairs Officer collected them at the airport and drove them to an apartment somewhere in the depths of Shijingshan. The apartments were shared by two teachers. Some of the teachers came as couples, but most did not. Two strangers would find themselves living together in this bewildering environment. Most of them became great comrades, but some grew to loathe one another.

After their first sleep in Shijingshan, Sam and the Foreign Affairs Officer would collect them at their apartments and bring them into the school. As they got out of the van and entered the courtyard, my giant head grinning down at them, they were typically full of trepidation. As they entered the school and saw all the staff in their red t-shirts, smiling and welcoming them, they would relax a bit. They were led upstairs to Finlay, for orientation and training. More often than not they were teaching before the end of the day.

Most of the foreign teachers who lasted delighted in the bizarre environment. Everything was different here, but it was always the little, unexpected things that were most shockingly so. Whenever someone new arrived, I could see it all first-day-fresh again, through their eyes. I was always hustling on thebeijinger and Dave's ESL Cafe for backup, and I was ruthless at times. I always made sure that I had more teachers than I really needed, and more waiting in the wings.

As soon as the September team was in place, trained up and ready to go, Chen Xi started laying on the beery banquets in remote mountain villas in Mentouguo. Chen Xi and Chen Fu always ordered an incredible variety of food which we spun around on lazy Susans, and boxes of beer were lugged in from the van by Sam and Fan Cheng.

Every table had *baijiou*, for those who dared. There were speeches and team-building activities, silly games, and laughter. Toward the end Chen Fu would get up and sing in grand, Mongolian style:

Lan lan de tian shang bai yun piao
Bai yun xia mian ma er pao

Blue sky, white cloud,

Horses run beneath.

It wasn't long before the new teachers were arranging their own banquets. Beer and food were so cheap at the local restaurants that the foreign teachers could eat and drink like kings. Every evening after classes the teachers would gather at the *dapiadan* around the corner from the school, outside a restaurant which they dubbed Much Taste. Most evenings we would press tables together in the middle of the *dapaidan*. The foreign teachers were getting to know Chinese food, and they each had a favourite dish, which they were proud to be able to order in Chinese. The staff would bring us our dishes and bottles of Yanjing beer with big smiles, and then hang around a bit, joking and laughing.

Some of the Chinese teachers would join us for a beer or two on their way home, but they wouldn't stay long. The Chinese teachers earned about a quarter of what the foreign teachers earned. We were always trying to get new foreign teachers to drink *baijiu*, and when one of them did there were great roars of encouragement, and the Chinese people around us would watch and laugh. After the other foreign teachers slipped away, Finlay and Tony would stay on drinking and chatting into the wee hours, and I sometimes joined them.

Some evenings we would go over to the KTV across the road from Much Taste. At first we got them to bring in a lineup of girls, but once we became regulars we would just ask for the usual country girls with no English. I would connect my mp3 to the speakers, and put it on shuffle. We danced and drank and laughed in the little rooms. The KTV girls seemed happy to be with us, although they never got extra tips. Sometimes I rolled up a reefer, but no one ever smoked it with me.

Hong Fei, Hudia and the other KTV girls called me Da Hui Lang, big grey wolf, and I encouraged people to call me this, even after I understood that it had the same meaning as big bad wolf. When I went into the KTV on my own, I would cry between joints, and Hong Fei and Hu Dia would stroke my back.

When a red banner appeared above the door of the KTV, one of the Chinese teachers told me that it said don't do illegal drugs. Da Bing, our local police contact, told me that they knew everything about me, but he said this in a way that was friendly and self-satisfied.

There was a lot of money coming in, but also a lot going out. Although their wages were very low, there were so many Chinese co-teachers that they became a significant cost. We had to keep raising foreign teachers' wages, to keep up with the current going rate. Also, when we gave Chinese or foreign teachers management responsibilities there was a pay rise involved. Chen Xi and I kept our wages in line with the foreign teacher's wages for most of this period.

Finances were transparent. We analysed Excel sheets of income and costs regularly, and then intensively in struggle sessions toward the start of a new term, as we calculated student renewal rates. All of the Chinese staff were involved in these meetings, as the bonus system was based upon student renewal rates.

Chen Xi purchased a white Honda Accord. She had to hire a driver also, because government people loved to party, and Chen Xi needed to involve herself in these circles, to keep our *guanxi* high. She was always dressed to the nines, and she loved big, designer bags. By 2013, we had over four and a half thousand students.

THE LEFTWARD PATH

After Chen XI moved out, and I was living alone in the apartment in Jie Shi Ping, I experienced vertiginous sensations of freedom. Nothing was true, and everything was permitted. I stood at the edge of my own glittering darkness, my inverted compulsions, and decided to give reign to my perversity. I loathed myself so much, felt such a need for abasement, such Dark Delight at the prospect of the obliteration of my masculinity. I was thrilled, my senses electric, edging toward total surrender.

I resolved to discover what had made me into this monster of suffering, what was at the bottom of my need to be nothing, to be abnegated, peripheral, mere witness to the Goddess of Beauty, mere supplicant to the Perverse Ideal. To never own, but to be owned, to claim no rights as a man, to be always a witness, and never a participant.

It was easier with Chinese women, who did not know the codes of romance as practised by westerners. When I had drunk the cup of my perversity dry, perhaps the hunger would be sated, and I would go back to Chen Xi and live a domestic life with her. I imagined it might be peaceful to surrender, sink into the Real.

One of the illegal taxi drivers who waited at the entrance to my *xiaochu* became known among the foreign teachers as the Dirty Driver. He told me that he loved sex but his penis was too small to give pleasure to his wife. He told me that his biggest grievance was that his wife didn't enjoy sex because of this. I still had very little Chinese, so it took a lot of rude gestures, and even some sketching for him to express this to me. He had a young daughter, of whom he was very proud, and for whom he would do anything. He sent her to Aihua, even though he couldn't really afford it. He was always asking me for discounts but Chen Xi wouldn't hear of it.

The Dirty Driver would take me into Sanlitun, and wait in the car while I went into the Bus Bar. I let him come in with me a couple of times, but when he went on a dander among the tables, thinking that any girls drinking in a bar with black guys must be prostitutes or porn stars, Andy asked me not to bring him in anymore. Sometimes after I was done at the Bus Bar I would just get a ride home, smoke weed and try to write a poem or something.

Other times I would dismiss the driver and engage in a disheartening liaison with a Mongolian lady, or join Benito and the French party animals at some underground techno club. I saw David Holmes and Paul Oakenfold, but the best nights were those with local DJs, like Chozie, Osami, Patrick Yu and Pancake Lee. Over thumping techno they looped and distorted Jim Morrison shrieking Hello! Hello! Hello! consolidating our time and place, and the whole crowd, yellow, black and white, was arms in the air and pogoing. Sweat on scalp, hair on end in the throbbing wave of sound, the crush of bodies, the rushes and cascades. I didn't have to be me at these times but I was also especially me, holding on hard to the core of myself through the gusts of techno, the sacred winds of self obliteration.

Jude, a Nigerian guy who said he was a preacher back home, would meet us at a little bar, like Kai, in Sanlitun, to deliver pills. I would find myself in a cab at 4 am, sneaking back between Tiananmen and the Forbidden City, under Mao's unsleeping gaze. When I was safely back in Shijingshan, I would have a little bamboo basket or two of *xiaolongbao* from one of the early morning breakfast guys, before going up to bed.

I had dinner with our new Foreign Affairs Officer, Molly Wang. She had excellent English and a studied accent. Before travelling to Beijing she'd focussed on improving her English by listening to recordings of Jane Austin novels, stopping the playback after each sentence to repeat it out loud. Her first job in Beijing was as an interpreter at an Australian-run golf course in the east of Beijing. Her boyfriend was a disabled

Australian guy of 60. The Australian boyfriend had a wife in Australia, and Molly was jealous of her. I told her about my book on Joyce, and began to weave a web around her. A few days after whipping me mercilessly with my belt as I knelt naked on the floor one morning before work, she collected her meagre belongings from the golf course and moved in with me.

At our next start of term party, Molly sat on my lap. I saw Chen Xi's mother and Aunt glaring at me. Chen Xi left early. I didn't want Molly on my lap; I was appalled by the lack of decorum, but it was hard to get her off, given the story I was weaving around us. She could get angry very easily, and she was prone to shouting and making a scene. When she was angry she knew how to make me suffer, and I had given her the tools.

Chen Xi hated me, and I often left her office with mugs shattering on the wall beside my head. She came to my apartment to collect some last things and noted Molly's leather clothes. I punched the imprint of my knuckles into the face of our refrigerator, and Chen Xi lifted a vase that John Liu had given us, and smashed it into the glass of our fish tank. The gush of water spread our glimmering tropical fish across the floor, where they lay fluttering, trying to breathe. I collapsed with my back to the wall and sobbed. Chen Xi came over and stroked my head and said she was sorry she had hurt me so much. I couldn't get out a word. She slipped out the door quietly. After a few days we went back to war.

Although most Chinese thought that Molly was ugly, and there was indeed an ugliness about her, when she was dolled up in a nightclub she was stunning. I took Molly out to Sanlitun, and encouraged her to meet other guys. She did this enthusiastically. It would thrill me at the start of the evening, but toward the end of the night when I was standing alone against some pillar drinking, I would become embittered and there were often scenes of violence.

The Dirty Driver would take us into Sanlitun, and we would start off in the Bus Bar, tracking down weed, and maybe some e. My Nigerian buddies at first took me aside to warn me to be careful of Molly, but then, when they realised she had my blessing, I was beyond the pale, and it was more difficult for us to be friends. Our next stop would be a techno night somewhere in Chaoyang with Benito and the Frenchies. We sometimes went back to one of their apartments for a party. The French guys would get cocaine.

On Saint Patrick's day I was invited to give a talk on Irish Literature at the Bookworm in Chaoyang. Molly and some of the foreign teachers came along. At the end I digressed to a new theory of mine, that reading literature is bad for you. It was trite and flippant– I was thinking about how I had used my reading of Blake and Joyce to bolster my anti-self and entrench my self destructive impulses in a mythology that rated intensity of experience above all else. An American guy who worked for *thebeijigner* called me on this, and I couldn't defend my argument, though Tony and Finlay congratulated me on the talk afterwards, and I thought it had gone well enough.

When Molly and I got home, I felt good about myself. Molly didn't like me feeling good about myself, and she started slapping me in the face. After a sharp slap on the bridge of the nose, I slapped her back, and fattened her lip. She dragged her red fingernails across my throat. I spent the rest of the night wrestling her out of the apartment, locking her out and being locked out in turn. She clamped her teeth on my inner thigh and wouldn't let go. It was agony, and I tried to pry her mouth open with my fingers. She didn't release her grip until the neighbours came out and intervened. By morning light she was trying to cut her wrists with a pair of scissors. I dragged them away from her and we cut both our hands. When I put them back in the sink they were smeared with blood. We tussled again, and then she sank down against the wall sobbing, in the very spot I had sunk after the incident with the fish tank, and just as Chen Xi had sobbed when she thought she had failed her exam. I felt that I had let so many people down, and the world was so heavy around me. I realised everyone carries their own immeasurable sadness, you just had to open your eyes to see it. I felt sorry for her and I wondered if I had been just to her. Her life was a frantic struggle. The spell was broken by her sadness: she was not something elevated, she was down in this shitty world with me. She lost her place of prominence in the paradigm of my perversity.

It was morning and we hadn't slept. We went to the KFC in front of Wanshan for coffee. Across the entire empty parking lot were hundreds of praying mantises. Inside the KFC, two young girls had a pair of praying mantis, and were playing with them like dolls. One of these kept turning its head to look up at me as I sipped my coffee.

When we got back to the apartment, Molly put makeup over her split lip, while I got dressed to go to Aihua. She was going to Chaoyang to do a modelling shoot. Molly's face from that morning remained on a billboard above a French barber shop for years after. The Sanlitun Frenchies were unhappy that I had hurt her lip. She was very popular in Sanlitun, especially among the techno set. Her love of music was so clear. Trance was her favourite, and when she danced she was like a liquid beacon of joy at the centre of the dance floor.

One Saturday night when there wasn't much going on we bumped into a French guy who said he'd like to buy some cocaine and party with us. He was an evil nerd with thick glasses and I knew he wanted to be able to say that he was the first of the French to come home with us. I dug up Jude for cocaine, got a bottle of whiskey and jumped in a cab back through Tian An Men to Shijingshan.

We staggered out of the elevator, and immediately started snorting coke, rolling joints, and drinking whiskey and beer around the coffee table. The whole affair was so wretched, so staged. I knew I needed to be up in the morning, and I knew how much I would suffer. The Real would pay the price for the excess of the Imaginary, and my planet would burn in technicolour.

Enthralled by the fantasy, I had become its thrall. I felt like standing up and saying, right, fuck off you, and you too, you wee bitch, but I didn't because I knew this was all of my own making, and that it was right that I should pay for it, though I could not conjure the fantasy to comfort me. This should have been a situation that filled me with dark ecstacy, but I felt nothing. We got into bed in our underpants, with Molly between us. I heard him kissing her. I propped my pillow up behind my head and became a corpse.

I woke up with a start at 8:00, and realised I needed to be at the finals of our annual Aihua Cup Rising Stars English Competition at 9:00. Molly and the French guy were dead to the world as I got dressed in my tweed jacket and tie. My nose was running terribly, and my eyes were blinking blinded at Rising Stars as I interviewed and bantered with hundreds of Chinese primary school children, one after the other, in an auditorium full of parents, teachers, headmasters and government leaders. I finished at 5:00 in the evening. When I got home and went into my room to change, I was surprised to see the French guy on top of Molly, fucking away. I left the room and went to the computer to look at the news or something. Molly came in and apologised, and the French guy got dressed and left. I didn't understand why

Molly was apologising to me. Living with Molly had become hell on earth.

I often called my father from the third floor. I stood in the corridor with a Nescafe 2+1, looking out the window and smoking while I chatted with him. It was my morning and his early evening. We talked about the old days, when we were a family in Calgary. He told me about his time in Africa, where I was born, and about growing up in Donegal. He often said that he was lonely. He and Netty were living in a cabin on Denman Island, and she would go to stay in Calgary for weeks at a time, leaving him on his own. When he told me his sister had finally passed away, I decided to pay him a visit.

Rosemary had lain alone in a hospital bed in the Omagh County Hospital, since their mother had died ten years before. She had severe MS, and she could not focus her eyes, speak or feed herself. She was a living corpse. Sometimes I tried to imagine how much suffering she endured. but I always had to turn away from this.

While my grandmother was alive she spent every day in the hospital with Rosemary. During her final years my grandmother talked all day long to Rosemary about things that had happened sixty years before, as though only minutes had passed.

After my grandmother died, I travelled to Omagh from Dublin by bus. My dad flew from Calgary and Peter from

Botswana. Together with John Chambers we carried her casket across the yellow backdrop of the Sperrins. The coffin was so light, and I thought about how many secrets were gone, about how no one really cared that they were gone, how nobody even noticed. Peter took the cavalry sabre that was the match to the short sword I had pilfered when I was thirteen. My dad and Peter sold my grandmother's house. They found a pillowcase full of bullets hidden in the attic and they handled these in to the police. My father flew back to Canada, and Peter back to Africa. We all forgot about Rosemary, who lay alone in a hospital bed for ten more years, unable to speak, see, eat, or move. The fabled inheritance from David Sydney Clements, my great grandfather, had been held for Rosemary while she lived, and now, with Peter dead of prostate cancer, it would be divided between my father and Peter's son, Moray.

I booked a flight to Vancouver, and when Chen Xi told me to have Molly out of the apartment before I left, we fought hard, although I knew that needed to happen. I just wasn't sure I had completed my penance. My flight from Beijing was delayed by 48 hours, and I spent this time in a hotel near the airport, provided by the airline. When we got to Vancouver, I watched the plane circle the airport on the flight-tracking map, and then move east, across the Rocky Mountains. As we came down in Calgary, I looked out over the southwest of the city, at the Bow River, at Edworthy Park. This is where I grew up.

When I was twelve, and I was starting to riot in fantasies of my own humiliation, my mother and I began to fight a lot. She came home one day and announced at the kitchen table that the doctor told her she had five years to live; we continued to fight for the five years she had left.

She was 39 when they told her she had cancer, and 44 when she died. In those five years she transformed from a beautiful woman to a shrivelled, groaning discard of pain. She would listen in on my phone calls and interfere in my life. She didn't understand how important the young ladies that I was on the phone with were to me, how everything hinged on their favour.

We fought and she pulled herself along a wall and cursed me, renounced the day she set eyes on me, went to stab me with a knife, really tried for my guts while I held up my shirt and said go ahead do it. She swung with all her might then collapsed in a heap, sobbing, broken.

I grabbed my jacket, ran out the door. So cold. Forty below. Went to Gord Pedlar's home. His parents were out and we hot-knifed in his tidy kitchen then went down to his room. I lay back on his waterbed. My jumper was tight at my throat. I blacked out and there was an old woman's claw at my throat then I was falling through hell, strata of fire and black as plain as day when I opened my eyes I was choking myself. Gord was standing looking down at me in dismay. His parents would soon be home he said, and he asked me to leave. So cold outside again I had to go home, sneak quietly into the house.

That was the last time I spoke to my mother. She was in the room above mine and she groaned in pain until the morphine hit. When no one was in the house I went up to see her once. Her skin was yellow and tight to the bone. She looked out at me but she was so far away I didn't know if she could recognise me. I said I will come back and rushed out of the room.

I didn't come back until she died on the night of Thanksgiving. I went up and saw her body small and sad. My dad said she sighed once and then was gone. I saw two men bringing her down the stairs in a chair. It was so long ago. My mother is dust now. She is not even bones. She was cremated so that they could take her back to Ireland, and place the dust somewhere there, in Tyrone.

We waited in the plane on the runway in Calgary for hours. I was feeling dark and heavy, and I had no luck in getting booze. The girls behind me were cute and I told them in Chinese I was going out for a cigarette. They encouraged me, *shi yi xiar*. I went to an open door and saw the dim Calgary sky opened up without the tint of the window, and I breathed in the air. There was a Viking security woman at the open door to the runway with heavy blonde braids and a taser at her belt. She would not smile or laugh. When the girls asked me if I'd had a cigarette, I told them yes, and did a pantomime of dragging at a cigarette between jolts from the taser.

When we finally got off the plane in Vancouver, I could understand what the people I overheard were saying, their words could insinuate themselves into my train of thought. I got a taxi with a Sikh guy to Horseshoe Bay, and then the ferry across to Nanaimo. It was evening again, and I sat on the deck smoking and drinking coffee, as light from the shore scattered across the undulating black water.

In Nanaimo, I got a cab to the Tally-Ho motel. Dan and I had visited a strip club called the Tally-Ho during our tree-planting days, and I thought this might have been the same place, but if it was, the strip bar was gone. I got a room, and was surprised to find that I was not allowed to smoke in it. They were very strict about this. I had a bottle of whiskey from duty free, and I got a few tins of beer.

I called my dad and told him I was in a motel in Nanaimo. He'd waited for me for eight hours in Nanaimo the day before. I told him about sitting on the runway in Calgary, and that I would see him tomorrow. I called Dan, and he said he would drive down, and be with me in about an hour.

Dan had been my brother Deane's best friend. They were a couple of grades below me in high school in Calgary. When we played Dungeons and Dragons Dan was always a dwarf, and Dean always an elf. I bullied them both, and they called me an ogre behind my back. We all hated Calgary; when they finished high school they went out to Vancouver Island to make their way.

I was stuck in Calgary until I finished my BA, though I went out to join them summers until I graduated, and then I joined them tree-planting, and we spent many an afternoon crashing through the rain forests with our dogs.

Deane had been working in Northern Alberta that winter as a jug hound for a seismic company. It was hard graft. He bought a van in Calgary and drove out to Vancouver Island. At my hotel room on Englishman River we watched *Hellraiser*. He drove on to Bowser, where Dan was living with Crystal on the stony shore.

I came out the next morning. I parked behind Deane's van and went in. Dan and Crystal were having coffee. Soon we were all laughing at how drunk they'd been the night before. Deane had slept in his van, and wasn't up yet.

We went out for a walk. There was a sea lion way out in the Strait of Georgia, blue mountains behind. The wind whipped our hair. Dan saw soot on the window of Deane's van. I opened the side door and went in. There was Deane at the back, sitting with his back to the rear door where he had slumped, trying to get out. I could tell right away he was dead. I didn't want to look more closely, so I got to the back and started trying to kick the doors open.

I heard Dan imploring from outside what are you doing? I sat down and looked at Deane. He was grey with soot. There was a bit of black blood in one nostril. The grey of his tracksuit was seared black at the thighs. His mullet head was hanging down. He looked so sad. Dan ran in and felt his pulse, and then retched and ran out. I started saying no, and then couldn't stop myself, saying no, no, not like I couldn't believe it but like I was insisting. After the police and the ambulance arrived and had taken the body away, Dan asked me to wash my face. In the reflection of the window was a terrible mask of soot and tears.

In the newspaper it said he had died from careless smoking, and they quoted my dad saying he hadn't firmed up yet on what he wanted to do with his life. That isn't what happened though. He was reading a book by candle light, and the candle fell onto his foam mattress, and as he tried to get out the back his sleeping bag went up, and this was enough fire to make his aerosol cans explode. My dad and Ralph put Deane's ashes in front of a bench they made by his cabin on Lasqueti Island.

Before the funeral, I walked around Westgate and Wildwood with walkman and headphones, remembering my cruelty to Deane.

Dan and Crystal went to Mexico, and I stayed on my own in their cabin smoking weed, walking and listening to music. I wrote by hand in blue notebooks. I was trying to write down everything that I could remember, starting at the very first memory, listing everything that had signified. I soon realised the impossibility of the task. Still, I had to fight, I didn't want everything, my mom and Deane, to be lost in time. I was festooned in ghosts.

I went to Dublin to do an MPhil in Anglo-Irish Literature, and ended up doing a PhD. Dan had gone to Nunanvit with his wife, Crystal, before returning to Vancouver Island, and now he was at the door, and we stood laughing at one another, at how we had grown up to be men.

I was twenty three when I'd last seen Dan, and now I was forty. He brought me a bag of Lasqueti Island bud, potent and stinky. This would do me for the week in Canada, supplemented by the nodge of hash Molly had stuck in my wallet, trying to get me in trouble with customs I guess.

We went out into the snowy garden and hooted and drank whisky and beer. Dan told me stories about going out on the land on snowmobiles with the Inuit, hunting caribou. I felt as though I was there as he told me his stories, his special Dan voice and crazy laugh. I was lucky that Deane had Dan as his best friend. I would never have made a friend like him on my own.

He asked me to come back to his house for the night, but I liked the hotel and we agreed that he would pick me up in the morning, and drive me up to Denman Island. I had a few more hoots and another tin of beer or two, watched a bit of TV. It had been a long time since I had seen TV, and it seemed so strange, the ads so insane.

Dan collected me the next morning in his pick-up truck. We listened to Horslips, stopped at The Boar's Head for a burger and ale, looking across at Lasqueti Island. My father had bought a cabin there after my mother died.

The island had no electricity, and the ferry was too small for cars. We would carry our packs two kilometres to find the right break in the woods to get down to the cabin. We spent much of our late teens and early twenties here. It started out as a rustic shack, but my dad developed it into a crystal palace, with vast, blank windows looking out across the oyster bay. When he married Netty my father sold this cabin, and the house in Calgary, and bought a cabin on Denman Island.

Arrived at Denman, we stood with my dad and Netty on their deck, looking across at the Coastal Mountains on the mainland. The mountain caps were covered in snow, clouds flowing over their shoulders. My dad had a hot tub on his deck, and as soon as Dan was gone, I got in and got the bubbles going. My dad brought me out a glass of his own wine, and set it beside me.

Slow, enormous flakes of snow were drifting softly through the still air. It continued to snow the whole time I was there. Trains of snow sat heavily on branches. These made a sudden cracking sound as they gave out beneath the weight. All my feelings of shame and regret came rushing back to me, big holes filling with icy water. I had to hoot and drink to keep these dark thoughts at bay.

My dad's hobby was making wine, and we would start in on the wine each day after lunch. Netty and my dad were very kind to me. The meals were great and the bed had many pillows. Dan spent a night with us. After it was dark and my dad and Netty were asleep we danced like primitive tribesmen to *Go Away*, by Cold.

For my return voyage, my dad offered to book me a seat on a water plane from Coquitlum to Vancouver airport. This would save me a day of bus, ferry and taxi. I always took for granted that my dad was flush, so I didn't think twice about accepting his offer. When I had my dad alone, I asked him about the inheritance from Rosemary. He was tightlipped about it, but when he was drunk once he said that it was a lot of money.

From the little window of the water plane back to Vancouver airport, I looked down at Lasqueti Island, at Maple Bay, and thought about all the places I had been, and how now I was on my way back home to Shijingshan. Chen Xi had succeeded in getting Molly out of the apartment in Jieshiping while I was in Canada, and over the coming months we achieved some balance at Aihua.

I was glad to be back in Shijingshan, until Finlay told me he'd decided to leave Aihua at the end of the term to take a job in Chaoyang. It was more convenient for him to get to his *baguo* training and the Sanlitun pubs from out there. He had done so much to hold the teachers together, and I worried about how I would manage after he was gone.

Also, I had a hard time not taking his departure personally. I got very drunk at the end-of-term-do, which doubled as Finlay's farewell party, and at the end of the night I wrestled him, and drove his forehead into the carpet. The next morning I had a fractured recollection of growling at him I'd eat ten of you, and Ray saying to me firmly, stop it David, that's enough. When I conjure this incident to mind, I see my face as the face of a snarling dog. The next evening at the *dapaidan*, Finlay was sporting a rug burn on his forehead, but he seemed to forgive me. He still sends me New Year's greetings on Wechat.

That evening after Finlay and the other teachers had left I stayed on at the *dapaidan* with the bottle of whiskey Muriel gave me as her going-away present. I was very drunk and the foreign teachers left the *dapaidan* one by one. Ray, who was taking over the role of Teacher Trainer after Finlay, stayed longest. I don't remember when he left.

A group of Chinese guys had gathered round me and were drinking *baijiu* with me while I finished off Muriel's bottle of whiskey. I didn't realise at the time that when the Much Taste staff asked them to pay they said I would pay. The staff wouldn't hear of this, and one of the guys at my table requisitioned the pot of *ma la tang* and was flicking boiling soup at the staff with the ladle, while the other guys were smashing dishes and hurling plastic chairs. I locked grips with one of the guys and the next thing I knew I was standing in the centre of the *dapaidan* with all the tables scattered, in the midst of a ring of staring Chinese people.

The police arrived and put me in a car. I kept telling the policeman dealing with me how handsome he was, and how good his English was. One of my buddies from the gym, someone high up in the police, came down and took charge of the matter. The restaurant staff were summoned to the station as well. They brought in the guy I'd wrestled, and showed me a bite mark on his forearm. He said he had a very sore back. Once it was established that I hadn't thrown a punch, they decided that I had acted as a hero in intervening on behalf of the staff.

Chen Xi and Madame Wang came down to the station to deliver me home. They were served tea, and they took the opportunity to get to know the police. I insisted that I wouldn't leave the police station until Cindy Pan, our new Foreign Affairs Officer arrived. I got another beer and drank it slowly, sitting out front of the station smoking while we waited for her.

I became obsessed with Cindy Pan. She was flirtatious, vivacious and hilarious. She lived with a boyfriend who was bald and had a neck like an ox. She would flirt with anyone but me. She had been warned about me, and she rebuffed all my advances, though of course the more she rejected me, the more obsessed I became. I had a file of photos of her, and I focussed the camera on her and zoomed in during teacher training. I would look at these photos and work myself into an erotic passion, conjuring her rejection and disdain. I was made to realise this was wrong when I showed Cindy Pan my secret file, and she was not flattered. She told Chen Xi and I was surprised by how upset they both were. Now I can see clearly why this was wrong, but at that time I could not.

Over lunch at a restaurant near Aihua, Chen Xi introduced me to Tan. Tan owned a company which produced e-learning material for Chinese children studying English. It was full of Chinglish, and Chen Xi asked me to help with the editing. I got some of the foreign teachers to do this. When Chen Xi suggested that we start using Tan's learning material at Aihua, I was against it.

Chen Xi also hired Tan to do an analysis of our company. Tan hung around for a couple of weeks and then gave his verdict to key staff at a meeting in the conference room. He concluded that the problem with Aihua was that it had two heads: Chen Xi's and mine. He drew a picture of a body with two heads on the whiteboard, and scraped an x over one of the heads. Chen Fu agreed with him, and I walked out of the meeting.

I thought Chen Xi and I had been getting on better, and she always assured me that Aihua belonged to both of us. When she asked me to sign divorce papers, I signed them without argument, although I didn't feel that there was any need for the drama. I still thought she would come back to me after I settled down.

Chen Xi was admitted to the hospital; she told me she'd had a breakdown because of all the pressure she was under. Madam Wang took me in the back of Sam's bus to see Chen Xi in the new Jing Yuan Hospital. She asked me to promise that no matter what Chen Xi told me I would not be angry. I couldn't imagine why she was saying this.

When we found Chen Xi in a hospital bed, she told me that she was pregnant with Tan's baby. I was crushed, and I sank down against the wall weeping. I was so alone. I could not catch a breath, or get a word out. I felt that everything was broken, and understood that it was all my fault. I had always thought that with Molly I had been sowing my wild oats, and that one day it would be just Chen Xi and me reaping the rewards of our mutual efforts. I'd thought one day I would be ready to renounce my hungers and lusts, and be content to live.

I held Chen Xi's hand as she cried, and told her that she would always be my family, and vowed that I would always protect our Aihua like a tiger. About a month later, Chen Xi lost the baby. She was devastated, and she was told she would never be able to have another.

When Aihua staff visited her in the hospital she could not stop weeping. I ushered the staff out of the room and sat down beside Chen Xi, held her small hand. I was so sorry for having betrayed Chen Xi so cruelly. My condolences rang hollow.

I felt like Chen Xi and I were closer after this. When she came back to work, our fights about the security of my position were less frequent. We had both faced enormous difficulties in holding up our sides of Aihua.

Chen Xi encouraged me to make a down payment on an apartment in a new housing block in Shijingshan. The development was reserved for local government and VIPs, so it would be very plush.

We met with John Liu and he got my name down for one of these apartments. We gave him a watch. I was still short about 10,000 dollars for the deposit. I tried to get a bank loan but could not. My ownership of Aihua had no legal standing, so I couldn't use this as collateral. I asked my dad to lend me the money, and Netty wrote me a long letter about how my dad was on a pension and it wasn't always easy for him to make ends meet. Chen Xi arranged for her mother to lend me the money.

Once, Chen Xi called me from a self-development retreat weekend, and she could hardly get a word out through the tears. She kept saying she was sorry, so sorry. I thought someone had died. When she recovered a bit, she told me that at the meeting they had asked her to think about someone she needed to say sorry to, and she had thought of me, and that was why she was calling. I was moved by this, and felt secure in my trust.

On Christmas Day, a group of the foreign teachers were going to Arabian Nights in Chaoyang for dinner. Cindy was going too. She had become very close with Eamon and Laura. I told her that I would not go, that I did not like Christmas because my brother had died at Christmas time. I thought if I told her this it would soften her feelings for me, and she would ask me to join them at Arabian Nights.

On Christmas morning I was as yet uninvited to the Christmas dinner. I went to the KTV across from Much Taste, and called Hudia and Hongfei into a room with me. I smoked hash and drank beer, then broke down in tears. They comforted me, and I left after a while.

When I got home, I was quite drunk. The pity for myself I'd evoked at the KTV was insufficient, mis-gendered, lost as I was, *among the strangers*. I called Eamon and asked him if it was alright if I joined them at Arabian Nights. I got a cab down and they were all at tables eating. Cindy was stunning in a turquoise top and dangly earrings. I called her out to speak with me for a moment in the foyer. I knew it was a very weak gambit, but I was desperate. I reminded her that my brother had died at Christmas time, and she told me that this was not her problem. I knew that this would be her reply, but I just wanted to hear her say it. This was the kind of reaction that would later give fodder my to fantasies about her indifference, but there in the foyer of Arabian Nights, with all of the foreign teachers looking on as I pleaded with her, it incensed me, and I told her that she was fired for the hundredth time in recent months. She laughed at me, and went back to Eamon and Laura, and the other foreign teachers celebrating Christmas. I got a cab home.

When I got home I phoned Lin Zhe, a newish receptionist at Aihua. When I first saw her at reception I thought she must be a spy planted by another school, she had such light in her eyes. When we were short of Chinese teachers she worked with me teaching kids at Shiyi Primary School, and I had taken her out for hot-pot after classes. She smiled as though at a secret when I ordered in Chinese. I asked Lin to come over, and within half an hour she knocked at my apartment door. We spent the weekend together, and over the following months she gradually moved in with me. She was distant and exquisite, so we sat together saying nothing. Perhaps she could pity one who was *lost among the strangers?*

Molly called me now and then, to let me know how she was doing. Sometimes I would get the Dirty Driver to take me around to her apartment near Chaoyang Park. I would give her a few hundred RMB, and then we would argue when she told me that she was going out on her own. I didn't want to get back together with her, but I wanted someone to go out drinking with. My sexual compulsion was now focussed on Cindy, who was utterly untouchable. Now that Molly was no longer my Mistress, I could feel pity for her, and this killed the possibility of lust. Her family was so poor and she had worked so hard to pull herself out of that life. If she fell she had far to go.

She was dating a rich Spanish guy now, who sold jet engine parts to Chinese companies. She bought a little apartment in Chaoyang, and often the reason for her calls was that she needed money to pay the mortgage, and I would help with this. When the Spanish boyfriend wouldn't, I took her to the hospital for the haemorrhoids he'd probably caused her.

Hanging with Molly kept the juices flowing. Once we were up on the balcony at Suzy Wong's and she was dancing at the bannister with a bevy of beauties, when a big English guy started pawing at them. I confronted him, and when he pushed me away I gripped his windpipe and had him pressed back over the bannister. The Chinese bouncers gathered and I let him go. He held onto the sleeve of my jumper, calling me Jedi, and insisting I step outside with him. He had the big hands of someone who does manual labour. I was aware of my limitations as a fighter. The Chinese bouncers got him away from me.

Just as I got out of a cab at Jieshiping, I got a call from Cindy. There had been a fire in Eamon McKermitt's apartment, and she and Sam were coming to collect me. Eamon lived with Lloyd Anderson, a bald, cartoon bouncer from East London. Eamon had come home very drunk, and made himself some sausages, but then fell asleep in his bed while they were cooking. Lloyd woke to the smell of smoke, and when he saw the fire in the kitchen he left Eamon in his bed and went down to get help. Looking at the apartment just after the firemen left, I was reminded of the smell in the van in which

Deane had died. There was a photo in the Shougang Daily of a Shijingshan Fireman in a helmet and breathing apparatus, carrying Eamon curled up like a baby out of the smoke-filled apartment. Chen Xi turned this into a PR coup, by sending Eamon and me around with a gift for the Shijingshan Fire Department, and having more photos taken. Eamon was exonerated and the blame passed onto Lloyd for having abandoned him to the flames.

At China Doll I would drink whiskey all night and parade my aggression, arms in the air. The owner liked to watch me get drunk, and he would sometimes send over a likely lad to test my mettle. I would notice some lumpy English or American guy dancing near me, but when I put on my evil face they would move away. One night at China Doll in the early hours Molly was flirting with a young Spanish DJ, and I felt I'd had enough. I pushed him across the room and onto a sofa. I lifted my fist as a gesture only but the Chinese bouncers grabbed me. We did a little Wing Chung routine and then locked grips. I told them in Chinese I would go right home, and that I respected them, and the owner told them to let me go. I ended up drinking into the wee hours of the morning for the amusement of the owner.

Whenever I went out to a club with Molly, I felt that people were sneering at me. When I went into work the next day, despite my tweed jacket, I knew I was a fraud. It became more and more difficult for me to advise our staff to be professional. I was two people. A passenger in myself, I was dragged to the bars and made drunk by my worst enemy. I would find myself involved in scenes of violence. The whole world was my enemy.

At a Sunday afternoon party on the rooftop of Kokomo, I was pissed off at Molly because she only came over to me for a drink from my jug of sangria. I grabbed her by the shoulders and shook her. She came back to me after a while and told me I'd better leave quickly, because the Russian guys at the table she was sitting at had said they were going to kill me.

When I said I would stay, she told me they had knives, and became more urgent. I could see that she was scared, but I wasn't. I was way too drunk. I switched from sangria to whiskey. I ran into the Dutch guy, Piet Bos, who'd made my Aihua Wordpress website, and had a few reefers with him at the bar. I met Piet in Maggie's bar during my first year in China. He was running a networking group called Young Professional People's Happy Hour. Now that the networking events had become more competitive, he was being squeezed out. He was teaching for Aihua part-time. I got him by the throat as we drank at the bar, because of problems with the website, but we ironed it out and kept drinking.

The next day when it was time for him to arrive for classes at Jing Yuan, he called me and told me he'd been beaten up by a group of Russians outside of Kokomo after I'd left. He was in the hospital now with a broken collarbone. He didn't come back to Aihua, and a couple of weeks later the Aihua website disappeared, and I had to build a new one on my own.

I went with Molly to a glitzy disco at Chaoyang Park West, a few doors down from Suzie Wong's. After a few whiskeys she told me that she had to go to Suzie's to meet her boyfriend. I stayed on and had a couple more drinks. As I went for the door, a regular of Suzie's, a Spanish gigolo with a six pack, grabbed a hold of me. He said a few words I didn't get, then started smashing his right fist into my face. I got him down and got on top of him, but I was down too low on his body. He was elbowing me on the top of the head. While I gathered myself to move higher up on him and get a hold of his throat, Chinese bouncers pulled me off. He got in another punch or two while the bouncers pulled me away. The elevator was all mirrors and going down I saw my face caked in blood. The white of my eye was red, and there were scrapes on my cheekbone and eyelid from his ring. The next morning Madame Wang and Cindy rubbed cream on my wounds. I never went clubbing in Sanlitun again.

During the final spasms of my adventures with Molly, I had been living with Lin Zhe. Lin was gentle and quiet, and it sometimes felt like I was living with a cat, or a ghost. It took me some time to recognise that she was the one I had sought all my life, and I took her for granted at first.

The last time I visited Molly, I brought her a computer game, Spore, on a hard drive, because she said that she was so bored, and we had shared an interest in computer games when we lived together. She knew that I was with Lin now, and she offered me sex, and told me that we could do anything I wanted. I didn't want this, and just tried to set up the game for her. Lin called and when I told her where I was, she insisted that I come back immediately. No matter what I said, she would only repeat come back right now.

I hadn't completed setting up the game for Molly, so I left the hard drive with her. All of my writing was on this hard drive, and I had no other copies. I never saw Molly again. When I later asked her for the disk back, she told me that her new boyfriend from California, DJ Ironman, who was the spitting image of Robert Downey Junior, had deleted everything from it to store music. She was also a DJ now, and had changed her name to Mo Bass.

DJ Ironman was working part time at Aihua. After he took an advance and quit, he tried to blackmail me with some compromising photos of me that Molly had filed away, but Molly told him David is not afraid of anything. I never recovered my writing and lost, again, everything I had ever written.

I bought a Hyundai Tucson, and got a Chinese driver's licence. I got 100% on the written test. Should you get out of your car and help someone injured? Of course not, roll up your windows and keep driving.

Lin and I would go out for drives in the mountains to the west of Beijing, in Mentougou. We often visited Cun Di Xia, a cliffside village. We went to the Silver Fox caves, near the Peking Man site with Colin Blance and Cherry Dou Dou. We got in a boat with a guide, and slid through the cave, and then we pressed through narrow passages on foot, twining downward. We saw the twisted white quartz after which the cave had been named, protected by plexiglass. We came next to a massive chamber, with stalactites and stalagmites at its outskirts. In the centre of this chamber was a movie screen and an old fashioned projector, playing Tom and Jerry. There was no sound, only the whirr of the projector in this deep space. There was a brightly lit fridge, and a bar, and the inevitable dusty Santa Claus. We sat down on plastic chairs and had a beer with boiled peanuts in the shell and hairy beans.

Once Lin and I drove two American teachers to the Mongolian border. Mike and Starla were too young for us to get them working visas, but they were good looking and bubbly and I knew they'd be excellent teachers, so I'd invited them over on tourist visas. They needed to re-enter the country after six months. For four hours leaving and returning to Beijing we sat in a crawling cue of blue coal-trucks, but when we got on the open highway running straight through the Gobi desert, we were the only car on the road. The world was flat and white. The road was perfectly straight, though gnawed away in places by drifts of white sand. The desert wind polished the car so that it was gleaming.

We came into an empty town through great concrete arches and cement dinosaurs. Lin and I waited while Mike and Starla went across the border in the back of a pick up truck. I had anticipated a grand Mongolian feast of roast lamb, but the restaurants were dire, and when Mike and Starla came back we just had a quick bite and then drove on. We did the trip in 24 hours without sleep, because we all needed to be back at Aihua. Lin and I got a cat, and it had kittens.

We moved to an apartment in Ray Da, to the east of Yuan Yang Shan Shui and the Sculpture Park. It was near where Dirty Street had been, but everything had changed so much, and Dirty Street was now a broad thoroughfare. It was great to get away from the neighbours who had seen me in my underpants with Molly's teeth locked on my inner thigh, and the print of my knuckles in the fridge.

The new apartment had a south-facing balcony and floor to ceiling windows. On Chinese New Year fireworks went off just outside our window. The people in the community worked in the Information Ministry just north of the community, and they were well-educated and polite. We got a huge, comfortable sofa, and a coffee table that was way too big. We got the biggest flat screen TV we could find, and I got an Xbox 360. I could get games for nothing at the DVD market. Rob Warman picked me up a nice guitar.

One day I was driving out of the parking lot at Wanshan, and I saw Lin on the road coming into the HQ, beautiful and smiling, in sunglasses. I pulled over and when I rolled down the passenger's window she told me was pregnant. I got out of the car laughing, with all of the cars waiting to get out behind me, and asked her what have you done? She joked that she was afraid she might have gotten pregnant in the Hualian swimming pool, and until we saw Davey's long, thin nose in the 301 Maternity Hospital, we both harboured a slight fear of this in the backs of our minds. Lin Zhe was the woman that I would at last give my life to. I had never hoped to have a child. I hadn't wanted to bring anyone into this world of pain.

bu dang jia bu zhi cai mi gui
bu yang er bu zhi fu mu er.

Unless you are in charge of a family,

you will not know the value of the things around you.

I began to understand how Ralph and Dan had become other people when they became parents, renouncing our boyhood dreams, forsaking our fellowship, forgetting all about Deane.

BRIEF FLOWERING

Aihua began to change in 2010, when we opened our Changyin Centre because we were no longer permitted to send our teachers into the Wuyi Public School. We managed to funnel many of the Wuyi students into our new centre, just down the road from the Wuyi school gates.

This new adherence to regulations happened first in Haidian district, and Wuyi was at the border of Shijingshan, on the Haidian side. We knew that eventually these regulations would also be enforced in Shijingshan. In 2012 we opened Zhongguancun Center in Haidian, around the corner from the largest primary school in Beijing. No matter how much we cleaned and tidied, there were giant cockroaches in the school each morning, until suddenly, for no apparent reason, this perplexing problem went away.

Guliu Primary School changed Headmasters, and the new guy didn't like us. He made it perfectly clear to me from the beginning that he did not have a word of English, and that he didn't want to have one. He kicked up a big stink about how I'd been throwing cigarette butts out the windows. He requisitioned our courtyard and we had to enter through his school gates and walk across the rubber playing pitch. At first he had the *baoan* stop the foreign teachers at the gate, but then relented in this decree. He only let our students in, though, and not the parents, and he dug his heels in on this.

Xi Jing Ping had begun his crusade against corruption, against Flies and Tigers, and there was no one we could turn to. We could not get our network of guanxi to reach this guy. We had another year on the contract with Guiliu Primary School, and we knew that we would not be able to renew.

The attitude to foreign people in Beijing began to change after the Olympics. I was always surprised to see how opinion moved in such a unified fashion. After the Olympics there was less of the Beijing welcomes you, and more of the *laowai*.

I think that the Chinese people felt a bit ashamed for having extended such a welcome to foreign people, like they had been duped again. Though China had celebrated the ideal of One World: One Dream, to them it seemed the west had not reciprocated, and they felt that China continued to be unfairly reproached and opposed. The welcome mat was withdrawn.

As I came to understand China more, I recognised that my schools were superfluous. I had always thought that China had something important to learn from Western culture, but I was wrong. In the West, the ideal of Freedom trumps all others. For the Chinese, on the contrary, the supreme ideal is Harmony, and any freedom should be in the service of Harmony. These are completely different ways of seeing the world, and of existing in the world. We in the west see the self as individual, actualised in particulars and details. The Chinese see the self as immersed in society, defined as a member of a group, a family, a work unit, a city, a nation.

Facebook, Trump and arguments over COVID masks and vaccinations show us that we should not be overly righteous in offering freedom and individuality pride of place as the highest ideal. I am not saying that it is not, just that we should not feel so certain.

It was easy to see why China banned Facebook, Youtube, Google and most western news sources. To have these sites available would undermine the Harmony of Chinese society. The west wanted to keep China down, and intentionally or not, these internet sources operated as soft power. They could not have been tolerated in China.

Who, apart from foreign teachers, would have wanted China to succumb to facebook anyway? We were all better off without it. Facebook was an opiate, and the Great FireWall may very well have preempted another Opium War.

Sanlitun, the bar streets in Chaoyang where foreign people ran amok, were bulldozed and replaced with up-market boutiques. Chinese guys drove through the squalid little corner that remained in the early hours, with bats and bars looking to batter any foreigners who were engaging with the local women. The Police were mostly indifferent when foreign men were beaten by thugs or by bouncers, and the general consensus was that they had gotten what was coming to them. Nigerian guys in Sanlitun were rounded up by Police with dogs, and those without visas were sent to prison for six months and then deported. There were clips of black guys sprinting and being pulled down by Alsatians. There was a general clampdown on street culture. Dapaidans were fewer. Dirty little street corners where people laughed and shouted over beer and street food were subsumed by shopping plazas, serenely marbled, and with upmarket boutiques.

Working at our HQ in Hualian, the business centre of Shijingshan, was very different from working at our school house in Gucheng. Hualian was east on Changanjie from the Amusement Park underground station, Bajiou Ditie. To the north of the station was Zhongchudaxia, where we'd had our first centre. To the south east at the left turn up to Laoshan was the restaurant in which Chen Xi and I had been married. It had changed its food style many times since I'd arrived in Shijignshan: barbecued fish, farmer food, Hong Kong food, hot pot, and now it was *malaxiangguo*.

Across Changanjie to the south of this restaurant was Jieshiping, two residential towers of 24 stories, where I had lived for most of my time in Shijingshan. To the west was the newly developed Wanda Plaza and Pullman's hotel.

I lived at Rayda, just to the east of Yuan Yang Shan Xiu, around the corner from the first place we'd lived in Shijingshan, south of Babaoshan subway station. Rayda was only nine stories, so it felt like there was more space around the community. It was connected to the Ministry of Information to the north, and most of the people living here were civilised and well educated. It was a pleasure to walk out among them in the evenings.

I would either walk or drive into Hualian each morning. When I drove there were long queues at intersections, people cutting into turning lanes, much honking and rancour. I entered the parking lot between Wanda and Pullman's through the barricade and could usually find a place to park if I came early enough. Otherwise I had to call down Sam or Fan Cheng to hang around in my car until a place opened up.

The stairwell and first floor elevators were at the entry to Meizhou's fast food floor, always crazy busy. There was a crowd of people jostling at the elevators. MeiZhou occupied the second and third floor, and the rest of the building was taken up by private education and small businesses. We were on the eighth floor.

If you turned left at the glass doors and reception, you walked down a windowless hall to reach our Admin and Marketing Departments, full of people who didn't speak any English. Chen Xi insisted on English names and put them on their name tags, but they often forgot what they were meant to be called. Chen Xi was Maeve for a while, but this never stuck. The desks were often empty, and the excuse was that they were on Center related business.

Chen Xi occupied the corner office, spending most of her time devising increasingly elaborate commission systems. The atmosphere in the rooms around her office felt secretive, cunning and unfriendly.

Chen Xi had assumed the title of President, and went on a hiring binge as soon as we took the offices in Wanshan. She wanted to build a team of professional people, but only succeeded in filling our offices with scammers and backstabbers. All of the people in these offices were new to Aihua. They had been assembled to help us franchise our school in third tier cities, and though they smiled and wheedled, there was no sincerity in them.

My office in the south west corner was the biggest office in the school. It had tall windows to the south and west. I had a big desk and a huge executive's chair. I spent months making a flow chart of our staff structure. So many people were coming and going and we had to be constantly shuffling and replacing people, making sure there were no holes. I presented these Staff Structure flowcharts in long and difficult meetings. It always became a struggle between Chen Xi and me. Nobody seemed to pay any heed, and the buck continued to be passed around.

From ten in the morning they began to flow into my office, one after the other, complaining of the shortcomings of their colleagues, and accusing one another of disloyalty and even treachery. Whenever I had a chance I worked on a plan for an online teaching system and student hub.

I read Vygotsky, and anything I could find on early learning. It was fascinating. Lin Zhe was expecting my son, and I considered how I could use all of this to benefit him. Once I started work on the online student hub we realised we had no central database of student records and set up a team to track these down.

Growth was rapid. Wanshan was also the fourth of our Centres, after Gucheng, Changyin and Zhongguancun. When we could no longer send teachers into Shijingshan public schools, we opened centres at YuangZhong, Jingdingdie Shijiecheng, Shenjing Guoji, and another around the corner from Guliuxiao Center.

All of our independent centres were designed after the principles of our Changyin Center. In 2009 we hired Lee Li and Kitty Meng, who urged us to brand ourselves as up-market, private education. When we lost access to Wuyi Primary school, we set up our first independent centre in an office building near the school gates at Changyin Daxia.

We hired a Feng Shui guy to work on the design of the new centre in Changyin. We had a fish tank at the reception, and the walls of the classrooms were glass so the parents could watch.

At Lee's advice we opened our next Center at Zhongguan-cun, around the corner from the gates of the biggest primary school in Beijing, and ran it according to the system in Changyin. Lee and Kitty stayed with us until Chen Xi and Kitty had a terrible shouting match, and Chen Xi fired Kitty. We could not get them to reconcile, and so Lee left also.

After Lee and Kitty left we continued to design our centres with glass walls through which parents could watch the classes, and interactive white boards. We branded ourselves as an upmarket teaching system with professional foreign teachers. Our classes were small, of eight students only.

The students were collected at the school gates by their foreign and Chinese teaching teams, and taken to the centre for lessons, or to sit and do homework in our library until their parents collected them. We had a lot of VIP students doing one on one lessons. The kids were not as adorable as they had been in the public schools. There were no more children of humble people in the mix. Now they were all of the Little Emperor variety, and the parents were demanding.

Of all the factionalism at Aihua, the most intractable was that between centre level management and HQ level management.

The most difficult position to hire for was Centre Director, and we had to change these people frequently. The Centre Director was the most important person for our success as a business, so it was a problem that they proved to be the least loyal to Aihua.

Each Center also required a Service Supervisor, an Administrative Supervisor, a Sales Supervisor, a couple of Course Consultants, a receptionist, a cleaner and a Senior Foreign Teacher. With the Centre Directors in constant flight it became difficult to keep people in any of these positions, and it even became difficult to keep Chinese teachers.

The Foreign teachers had become the most stable aspect of Aihua. Although they usually stayed only a year or two, they would finish with us according to the terms of the contract. We had fifty full time teachers with us, on our visas, staying in accommodation provided by the school. David Cooney, of Teachers for Asia, was helping me to source teachers now, and the standard of the foreign teachers had improved. There were fewer of the lost young men, although there were still some in our ranks. Most of the foreign teachers intended to make teaching their career. They were all in their mid to late twenties - cool and good looking, like a team of models.

They hated to be sent out marketing around school gates, but we needed them to do this before the start of every term. We handed out blue, cloth Aihua bags, with promotional material inside. We taught the teachers how to make balloon animals, to get the kids over, so that the Chinese teachers could start selling.

I would sometimes join in to show the foreign teachers how it should be done. It was mostly the grandparents who collected the kids from school. I would approach a grannie or grandpa and hand them one of our blue bags, telling them in Chinese how very useful these bags were for carrying cabbages. I would spread out my arms like Jesus, saying in the voice of a familiar advertisement, Wo Men Shi Aihua Ying Yu Pei Shun Zhong Xin, and pass them a bag. The foreign teachers stood in little knots, watching my antics sceptically.

The final Aihua banquet was for the tenth anniversary of our licensing to hire foreign teachers. We held the party on the main floor of MeiZhou and had about 300 people in attendance. Against Chen Fu's advice, Chen Xi spent a lot of money on this party. She invited government leaders in charge of public education, private education, and foreign expert certification. We invited all the winners of the Rising Stars Aihua Cup English competition.

I invited Declan Kellegher, the ambassador of Ireland, and flanked by several Chinese girls in ornate *chipas*, I led the ambassador and his wife from the carpark up to the celebration. Chen Xi gave a speech in a blue ball gown, Declan Kellegher gave a speech, and some of the Chinese government people gave speeches. I did not give a speech but I had the seat of prestige at the front, centre table, facing the stage.

We had Chinese acrobats, dancers and singers. The foreign teachers put on an excellent performance. There were talented people among them. Rob Warman played guitar and sang a Chinese song. Jonathan Chatwin played guitar and sang *Blowing in the Wind*. All of our teachers, English and Chinese, sang Stand by Me together.

We'd always had a special advantage going into the public schools. Now we had to face our competitors on equal footing. The private education sector in Beijing had become much more competitive. There were so many students, and so much money to be made. When a school owner ran away to Canada with millions in prepaid tuition, it freed up students for some of our centres, but it also made regulations more strictly enforced. The writing was on the wall. From her government contacts, Chen Xi had begun to hear whispers that there was no future in the Private Education Industry in Beijing.

Despite struggling to keep key members of staff, Aihua was making a lot of money. Chen Xi had put aside money to support our efforts to franchise the school in second and third tier cities, and the online students hub and learning system I was developing. She and I were earning 40,000 RMB per month, and we were giving ourselves a decent yearly bonus. We only needed to keep the whole thing together.

10,000 YEARS OF HISTORY

Just before Lin Zhe discovered she was pregnant, my dad told me Ralph, Sam and their kids would be visiting him that summer, and it might be a good chance for us to all be together. Who knows, he said, when we might have another chance. I decided to visit him on Denman Island that summer, and began looking forward to it.

A few weeks later, my dad called back and said that Netty's daughter, Crystal, and her husband, Jason, would also be there that summer, and that it might be crowded if I came also. He suggested I come another time. I told my dad that I would never speak to him again. In an exchange of emails with Ralph, I realised that he and Sam were complicit. My dad phoned the next day and apologised, and we agreed that I would visit that summer.

He booked me a seat on a water plane from Vancouver to Comox Valley Airport. I brought 700 Canadian dollars, and left my bank card with Lin. I wanted Lin to come with me, and if she had, everything would have turned out fine. She would have been three months pregnant by the time of our flight, though, and we decided it might not be good for the baby.

I turned up at my dad's cabin with an extra-sized bottle of Black Bush. Ralph, Sam and their two kids, Grace and Fergus, were already there. Ralph made it obvious that he didn't believe my story about the Russians in Kokomo, and I overheard him joking about this on the phone with Dan.

Ralph and Sam's kids needed to sleep in the room with my dad and Netty once I arrived, and Sam suggested I might be happier in the little shed away from the cabin. It probably would have been a good idea, but I told her that I didn't want to do this. I was smoking heavily, and Netty gave me a special place to throw my butts. She said they left a smell in the kitchen when I dumped them in the bin.

Dan arrived the next day with a bag of skunk. Ralph, Dan and I set in on the whiskey and weed. I brought out Nettie's speakers and DJ'd from my MP3. After everyone was asleep, we got into the hot tub. When we ran out of whiskey we opened bottles of my dad's home-made wine. Ralph and I didn't agree on the music. He wanted to hear the Pixies, but I played Tupac. It is not really my taste, but I had been getting into *Starin in the Rear View Mirror*. Netty came out and asked us to turn down the music a bit.

For some reason, when the sun was coming up, Ralph and I were standing out of the hot tub and I was telling him I am a thug. I'd had sleeping pills on the plane which had really knocked me out. Maybe this was partly to blame. He was telling me with scorn not to stand there puffing up my chest at him, and my dad came out in his bathrobe and told me David, that's enough. I will forgive you, but that's the last time.

Ralph went to bed and Dan slipped off into the woods, as he usually did in such situations. I played Hawkwind, *Master of the Universe*, the slow building roar, and shadowboxed on the deck until I was exhausted. I slept for the better part of two days, and woke wondering who and when I was.

When I was up, Sam suggested I should book my return journey to Vancouver airport now, so that I didn't have to do it at the last minute. When I didn't show any initiative in doing this, she offered to call the bus station or the water plane company for me. She and Netty didn't want my father to pay for another water plane ticket for me. When she was calling me, saying, Dave, I got through to someone, and waving the phone at me, I slipped down the steep pine slope to the gravel beach.

I sat down with a beer and a reefer looking over the oyster shore to the mountains on the mainland, which were dark blue, and with clouds pouring over their shoulders. The tide was out and the shore was sizzling with life.

I made this the time and place where I discovered the time machine in the story I wrote after we sold Aihua. The time machine was a flying bed that could also be a submarine, which I had imagined to help me sleep when I was young. I could go to any point in the past with this time machine, and I had a suit that could make me invisible. I could alter events, but then whenever I slept the day was reset, and unless I travelled to another point in time I stayed at this day undergoing a series of groundhog days.

It was a Block Universe. There was no paradox to deal with. When I slept the day would reset; but I knew that the changes I'd made continued on in alternative universes I had sheared off from ours through my actions, and which, through laws of parallax, shot away from ours.

I had a lot of poorly written adventures in the time machine, but it all led back to my mother. I was trying to rescue from oblivion the last time she smiled. My mother had been beautiful and kind. She was childlike in her happiness. This was lost behind so many years, and one day it would be even less than a memory. I could not allow this obliteration of her laughter to become absolute.

Sitting there at the edge of the sizzling oyster bay, I wondered who Deane was. Who was my mom? I knew they had been more than the source of my remorse. I wondered who they might have become, what lives they might have lived, and it was this question that necessitated my discovery of the time machine.

Deane was a young guy who hadn't yet firmed himself up as to what he wanted to do with his life. It was terrifying for all of us then, as we gauged to what level we would need to stoop to earn a living, what clownish hats and what collars we'd need to don to evade destitution. It was humiliating to come to understand that one day to put food in our mouths we would have to be tame dogs dancing. For such as us, the step from boyhood into manhood demanded complete renunciation of the self, and utter fraudulence.

Deane was tall and wore a mullet, a Siberian Tiger-striped muscle shirt, and a feather earring. He would definitely have had a few tattoos by now, had he lived. He loved to party, and when he was too drunk, he swaggered like a rock star. He was friends with many, never the cool guys, but always the little losers at the periphery. He was humble, though he didn't really need to be. It must have been a middle-kid thing.

Dan had found in the van a seared, blue folder of loose leaf paper in which Deane had been writing a story by hand. I still have it with me, here in Galway. It is one of the few things that have travelled with me around the world. A little while ago I took the time to type it up. It was called Fillardy Goblin. It wasn't very good. He was only twenty.

The story took place around the goblin campfires. It was the world of the bonfire parties kids from our high schools had in the hills and forests around southwest Calgary when we started to drive and drink. I never went to these bonfire parties. They were for heads, and I was a jock. We had our stoned, drunken gatherings in Kevin Whitfield's basement, listening to the Cars instead of metal. The bonfire parties were rough, boozy affairs, and Deane captured this in his story.

Fillardy was a little, wimpy goblin, but he was smart and realistic. He was an exaggeration of Deane's humble side. He hung quietly at the edge of the party, but he was the guy who had lit the best fire. Another goblin took credit for the lighting of his fire, and he said nothing, to avoid confrontation. The goblin who took credit for Fillardy's fire was probably me. Later though, the opportunity arose for Fillardy to prove his courage and his worth.

The story stopped there. Maybe it's best that he's gone. It takes so much to love with all this dying.

If my mom could have existed in the world with the hot tub and my dad making wine in his happy retirement, and we could have gotten along, and forgotten about all of the terrible, hurtful words said during that time of dying; she would be sitting, smiling in a deck chair in the sun, a sun bonnet on her head, hummingbirds around her, chatting about her childhood, making fun of people, imitating their voices.

My mother was neurotic, and she had so many debilitating phobias, but she could be charming and funny. She missed her twin sister, Willow; they exchanged handwritten letters that took two weeks to get there. Her fear of flying cinched her even tighter in exile and despair.

She was locked up in a little house in the suburbs all day, but was terrified of being in a car, and never had the slightest intention of learning how to drive. These suburbs and malls were not what she considered to be life. Before all of that though, I remember she was like a girl, my mother, remembering Ireland. I remember so far off, almost at the very edges, the very limits of my memory, her gorgeous laughter, the warm glow of her smile. All of time is tearing this from me, as it even tears me from myself, relentless, breathless black metal winds. She was beautiful, my mother. It is so hard to remember.

I focussed my memory on a time before the terror and rage. I had come home from school feeling awful about being called chicken and chased home by boys on banana-seat bikes. I sat down on my bed, sobbing. She came into my room and sat down beside me. I watched as if from the corner of my room.

There I sat, ugly and futile. Yet she had loved him, borne him in her arms and in her heart. But for her the race of the world would have trampled him underfoot. She stroked my trembling back with her gracious hand, though I remained inconsolable.

For the rest of my stay at my dad's cabin, I retreated behind a haze of smoke. I sat writing obsessively in a black journal. Netty remarked wryly that she would love to know what was going into my little black book. I think once when I went out she and Sam discovered where I'd hidden it. I was writing very hardcore pornography about being Cindy's slave, drawing her scorn and disdain. I don't know why I was writing this then and there as though my life depended on it. I suppose I thought this might protect me from actually being there and then.

One morning I took Ralph's daughter, Grace, kayaking. She was six or seven I guess. My dad stumbled after us along the shore, his weak ankles sliding over big round stones. I knew Sam had asked him not to let us out of his sight.

After dinner there was a row between Sam and me over the use of my dad's van, and my dad sided with Sam. I told them I would leave. I packed my bags and called Dan to collect me, but the last ferry had already left the island. It began to rain. I saw my dad searching through my bags, which I had left outside. When I asked him about this, he said he worried that my things would get wet.

I got drunk and then I took my bags back into the room I'd been staying in. I went looking for my boxes of books. I wanted to have them shipped to China. My dad told me they'd been damaged when the shed they were in was flooded, and he and Netty disposed of them. I didn't believe him. I imagined they hadn't brought them from

Calgary. There were a lot of books, all excellent and useless.

I played badminton with my dad. He didn't try to rally, but kept spiking the birdie down into corners. This had always been his thing. He didn't seem to get that other people could just spike it down too.

Afterwards, we sat down on a bench in the luminous green watching Ralph's kids playing. Having given up, I said, they are so privileged and so lacking in compassion. I was thinking about the kids at Aihua, and all the space and beauty that Ralph's kids had here, the shadows of leaves, the green light brimming on the lawn. My dad said ah, David, I always respected you. When he said this I mostly thought of the but, and the word he left out.

I loved and respected my father, but I think I resented how he had treated my mother. He was never a mean person. He was always kind and gentle. I never once heard him yelling. He was a man of his time; he shot beautiful animals in Africa because it was what a fellow was supposed to do, and dragged my poor, sick, beautiful mother from the only place she'd ever really known to somewhere she could not accept.

Then, how do you love someone who is dying? How hard it must have been for him to sleep beside her mortified body every night, as one surgery after another took away pieces, and her groans of pain became ceaseless. They were too young to have had the wisdom to face down dying. How hard it must have been to find memories of his beautiful wife. Once, a woman called on the telephone and asked for him. My mother asked who is calling, and the caller hung up. How could my mother have been anything but alone in her dying? Now, here he was treating Netty like his queen.

On my last night at dad's cabin, after everyone had gone to bed, I sat outside on the deck drinking beer and hooting. Sam came out and plopped down in front of me. She said, right, we need to have this out. I said that I was enjoying the quiet of nature for the last time before heading back to the bustle of Beijing, and that the last thing I wanted to do was have it out with her. Sam said I was a vile creature, and that she would do anything she could to protect her family from me.

The next morning, I told my dad about this as I put my bags in the back of his van. He said, wearily, oh David, you'd better just go. I snapped at him, I am going, that's why I'm putting my bags in the back of your van. I didn't go in to say goodbye to Ralph or their kids. I had to borrow twenty bucks from my dad to get smokes and have some change in my pocket. I remember our last shared glance at the airport, the sorrow in his eyes.

I posted on facebook that I would never return. Nick Georgosis commented that Elvis had left the building. When I got back to Beijing I sent a group-email declaring that I would never speak to any of them again, no matter what, death or birth. I received no reply from Netty or my father. I exchanged ugly, accusatory letters with Ralph and Sam. I think now that my dad knew he was dying and that his purpose in having us over was to say goodbye, but everything is uncertain.

Now my exile was complete, and I seethed in bitterness for weeks. Lin Zhe and I went to her hometown to be married. We flew to Mudangzhang and then got an illegal taxi to Lin Kou, where we stayed in a grimy hotel, the best there was, and travelled in the daytime to the little village where her family lived.

There are two Chinas. The world of Shanghai and Beijing is very different from the world of the small villages. Lin hates when I talk about her hometown, which is situated between North Korea and Siberia. I have never been anywhere that life was so poor and so hard. Her family couldn't understand my Chinese, and her mother and father were utterly alien to me.

I felt uncomfortable in the little shack in which they lived, with its *kang*, a cinder block bed they lit a fire beneath in the winter, and which also served as sofa and dining table. The roof was of corrugated iron, and they had yellowed pages of newspapers plastered to the cinder block walls. There were centipedes such as I have never seen before, with long, jointed legs. Everything was poverty and grime.

I went out for a walk and people peered at me through the slats of their blackened fences. They were not jolly, like the people in Beijing. The shack was set amidst a handful of others, and railroad tracks ran between these and a sprawling cement factory. A ways beyond this there was a poisoned little river, its water a luminous yellow.

The wedding ceremony was in a local restaurant on the single street that comprised the centre of the town. This street had the feel of a Spaghetti Western, dusty and heavy with dread. It was hard to imagine it was the same sun that lit this place.

Lin's school friends and family attended the wedding. We bowed to Lin's father and mother at the front of the room. Modest people, their faces remained sad and inert. We went around lighting cigarettes and drinking with guests. The people did not attempt to banter with me. There was a commotion when someone came in the back door and stole a crate of soft drinks. After a lot of screaming and shouting on the road, the drinks were retrieved.

Lin's brother-in-law made the mistake of trying to drink with me. It wasn't long before his face was glowing red, as some Chinese people's faces do when drinking, and he had to be taken home.

Lin and I flew to Harbin the next day, and hurried around government offices in the freezing rain to make the marriage legal. I was very happy to get back to my big sofa, my Xbox and Aihua.

At the 38th week of Lin's term, the doctor told her that the baby's heart-beat was elevated, and suggested she should come into the hospital to stay for two days before they would induce the delivery. I planned to name the baby Aragorn. Lin's mother took the first train down to Beijing in a hard seater. She wouldn't let us waste money on a flight, or even a soft seater.

As I drove from the hospital to the apartment to collect some things for Lin, Ralph called me from Australia. He told me dad had had a serious stroke, and that things weren't looking good. He said he was going to get the first flight he could to Canada. I told him that Lin was going to have our baby immediately, and that I couldn't come now.

A few hours later, as Lin's mother prepared *jidangeng* for Lin in our apartment, Netty's daughter, Crystal, called me and told me that my dad was dead. Lin's mother stroked my back as I sat on the oversized sofa and sobbed. Lin's mother stayed in the apartment because only one person was allowed to attend the delivery, and I went back to the hospital with the *jidangeng*.

When I got back to the hospital, they had moved Lin to a little room in the basement. It had the feel of a carpark. There was nobody down there, except a nurse who sat in another room looking at her phone.

Whenever I went up for a cigarette outside by the bins in the black rain, I tried to call Netty and Ralph, but they did not answer. Lin was wracked by waves of pain, and she shouted out that she could not do this, that she was going to die. I tried to get the nurse to do something, but she only told us that everything was normal, that it was supposed to hurt. Between her waves of pain, Lin and I sang *Silent Night*.

On a cigarette break, standing in the rain between the bins, I got through to Netty. I asked her what had happened and she told me my dad had woken up and found he couldn't read the numbers on the microwave, and didn't know how to use it. He knew that he should know how to use the microwave, but he didn't. Netty took him to a hospital, and he tried to fight off the doctors. They sedated him, and he died a few hours later from a massive stroke. Netty was in a hurry to get off the phone. She said she could not talk about this now. My face was wet with rain, and it was seeping through my jacket. I went back to Lin.

In the morning a doctor arrived, and Lin asked her to perform a caesarean section. She said she could not bear the pain. I supported the caesarean section because I wanted Davey to be born as close to my father's death as possible. I was surrounded by people who said that my father's soul would fly to Davey, and there was a small part of me that wanted to believe in this. I wanted to give his soul a body to land in after its flight across Alaska and Siberia, from Vancouver to Beijing. Lin was taken to an operating theatre and I waited with her friend, Li Yue.

When they brought Davey out wrapped in a blanket and with a little blue hat I could tell right away that he was my son. When we were all in the hospital room I read William Blake, Yeats, and the last pages of *Finnegan's Wake* to Davey, carry me taddy as you did through the fair. I could never read through the last two pages of Finnegan's Wake without choking up, I don't know why. The finality of going back to the sea and maybe being born again, after all that journey, I suppose.

Chen Xi was on a Management Training program in another city. When I called and told her my dad was dead and Davey was born, she was upset that she hadn't been there for me, and she travelled back to Beijing immediately. I had imagined the doctors agreed to perform a Caesarean section because my father had just died but in fact it was because the umbilical cord was twisted. Sometimes you can have no idea of what is actually going on around you.

That summer, as always, we had a number of summer camps on the go. We were also running Tan's summer camp, for students recruited from outside Beijing. Chen Xi was in Ireland leading students on our International Summer Camp. I had eight foreign teachers at Tan's summer camp in Fengtai, south of Beijing.

This summer camp was in a surreal aerospace academy in the middle of nowhere. Military cadets offered afternoon programs for the students. It was pouring rain, and Lin and I had just got Davey to sleep when Dwayne, a foreign teacher from Alabama, called me from the camp. He said there is a flood, Sir, and we require immediate evacuation. I asked him to put me onto Christy, the Senior Chinese Teacher in charge. He said negative, Sir. I cannot do that. We are in the mess hall with the students. The room is full of water and we are standing on tables.

I called Tan, and he picked me up in his silver Mercedes. We tried to drive down to the camp, but the bridges were flooded. We drove back and Tan dropped me off at my apartment. I got through to Christy, and she told me the cadets had waded through the flood and tied rope along the way to the dormitory, then led the students and teachers along the rope. They were now all safe on the second floor of the dormitories. I called Tan and he told me he was already on his way to the summer camp. I asked him to come back for me, but he said the headmasters of the summer camp students were in the car with him and there was no room. When I insisted, he said I had a new baby, and I needed to be safe.

I called Sam and told him to take me to the camp. He argued that we couldn't get there, but I was adamant. We worked our way through backroads in the Aihua van and as we neared the camp there were household articles bobbing in pools at either side of the road. People were wading through these pools, scavenging.

The summer camp now sat in the centre of a lake. Soldiers were ferrying students from the camp to the road in rubber dinghies. The headmasters Tan had driven down were standing around Tan's Mercedes. They told me that Tan had waded across, so I waded also. The water was opaque with mud, and I couldn't see what was beneath my feet. Plastic toys floated past me.

When I found Tan I got Christy to translate while I berated him. I told him that this was an Aihua camp, that Aihua was my school and my responsibility. When I told him that the foreign teachers were my charges, he told me he thought I should be more concerned for the students. I glowered at him in outrage, brought all of the power of the gaze to bear upon him. I looked at him exactly how I imagined beautiful women looked at me. He said OK, Aihua is your school, after this I will have nothing to do with Aihua.

I found the foreign teachers, helped students and teachers pull their bags out of the knee-deep sludge. Laptops were ruined, and I had to wrestle a wardrobe to free their bags and their clothes. I suddenly thought of all the shit that must be floating in this water.

Lin stayed at home with Davey, and when I got home from work, we would take Davey out in his blue buggy, to feed the cats. We first noticed Da Huang, a big ginger cat, poking his head through a wall and meowing intensely. After we started feeding him, Hui Hui, a big, grey cat, began to approach. At first he and Da Huang would arch their backs at one another, giving menace, but when they realised there was enough food to go around they ignored one another.

We discovered more cats in the tree-shaded courtyard behind our building. When we entered and called we were greeted by Little Pretty, Little Crazy, Little Bully and the rest of the tribe. As we promenaded around the building complex we would stop and let Davey run around with Mimi and Ray Ray while we chatted with their grandparents, and then Cheng Cheng and his dad, before going for dinner at one of the local restaurants.

I'd exchanged angry emails with Ralph and Netty for a few weeks after my dad died, and then there was silence between us. I was so upset that I could not sleep. I lay in bed examining the ways in which I thought they had done me wrong, and how this was intolerable, my head full of coiling, black snakes.

I'd always assumed that when Davey was born my dad and I would be reconciled. I'd imagined visiting Denman Island with Davey and Lin, and my dad playing with Davey while Lin looked on and hummingbirds whirred. I felt sad that they would never meet; my first memory was walking with my grandfather through the small forest at the back of his garden. He pulled up a huge stone to show me the insects wriggling in the dark beneath. The past too is hidden beneath a stone, and when you turn it over you reveal a creeping, crawling profusion of alien lives glistening blackness. He led me to little plants, and lifted leaves with two fingers to reveal red strawberries beneath, introduced me to the taste of white currants.

My grandparents' house was in Gortmore Gardens, beside the slow, black Strule. My grandmother told me stories of bodies floating past. They had two dachshunds, Hans and Mitsy, and I knelt by them while they ate and she told me not to put my face too close or they would bite it.

She offered other scary advice. She told me to never stick my head out the window of a car, because a lorry could drive past and take it clean off. She advised me not to drink from a bottle when in a car, because if you stopped suddenly the bottle could go right down your throat. I melted toy soldiers in their fireplace. My grandfather made me a submarine out of cardboard boxes.

My grandmother slept on the sofa, and I slept on an army cot beside my grandfather's bed. To help me sleep, he told me the story of Icarus. When I woke there was a bottle of lemonade beneath my pillow. This week that I spent with my grandparents is the first memory that I have. I only met my grandfather that once.

When we were living in Calgary, my dad received a phone-call saying his father had died and I saw him crying. My dad flew back to Omagh for the funeral and it was very difficult for my mother to be left alone with us three boys.

Ralph sent me a two page summary of my dad's life, which my dad had written in anticipation of his death. He told of his excitement standing on a hill in the evening, watching the Luftwaffe bomb Belfast in the distance. He spoke about being sent to the coal-shed during religion class at the Catholic primary school in Glenties, and how this was fine with him because he had a couple of toy soldiers in his pocket. He said that his time in Africa was the best time of his life. He didn't mention that he'd had to leave Africa when I came along, but it was implicit. For days after reading the letter, I was disturbed that my father had summarised his life in two pages.

When I broached the subject of the will with Netty she was livid. I told her that I wanted the leopard, zebra, and gazelle skins, and the elephant tusks. I was born in Africa, and I wanted my son to have this history in his house. When Netty told me that my dad had gifted these to her, I told her that my father had given them to my mother long before he had gifted them to her. Netty had her lawyer write to me, saying Netty wanted all future communication to be conducted through the lawyer.

Ralph MC'd a celebration of my dad's life on Denman Island, and then flew to Omagh with the ashes, where they are interred somewhere near my mother's. Netty's lawyer said that she would only send me my portion of the inheritance if I would sign a waiver stating that I renounced my claim to anything else. I didn't sign this waiver, but the check arrived a few weeks later anyway. It was less than I'd dreamed but more than I expected.

A few weeks after this a box which Ralph had organised for me arrived at Aihua. It contained a few books, including a

Topographical Dictionary of Ireland, and a black wooden carving of a Daoist with an *erhu* and a frog, which Willow told me an ancestor had brought home to Ireland from China a hundred years ago, that short sword that I had stolen from my grandmother's attic when I was thirteen, and my grandfather's shillelagh.

At the end of a week of blue-sky-days contrived by the Communist Party, there was a military parade down Changanjie. We stood just under the overpass of the Fifth Ring-road, right at the point where the parade turned around to travel back down Changanjie the other way. I had seen my share of goose-stepping in China, but now it was not on TV, and not just the kids in the Guliu Primary School. While I felt terror watching the ranks on ranks of implacable, inhuman faces, identical in purpose, my wife and the Chinese people massed around me at the white, cast-iron barricades, felt protected. Davey, perched up on my shoulders, hanging onto my head, was too young to comprehend what he was seeing. There were missiles, rockets and radar trucks, and jets in formation flew overhead.

Davey had only a Chinese name on his birth certificate, Lin Sheng Bo, and when I talked to the Irish embassy, they said if I got Davey baptised, the baptismal certificate could be used to get an English name on an Irish passport. I visited Martin Loftus, a Catholic priest from Ireland, at his apartment in Chaoyang. I talked to him about my bereavement. I told him I wanted Davey to be baptised at the Catholic Church. When he told me Davey would need to have a Catholic parent to be baptised in a Catholic ceremony, I asked him to help me become a Catholic. I told him I'd done my doctorate on Joyce, and read Dante, but he didn't think it was a good idea.

He put me in touch with a United Church, that was mostly Africans and Americans, and had a female minister from New Zealand. I attended a few services, and then I brought Chen Xi and Tan in with Davey and Lin, and they became his godparents, his *gan ma* and *gan ba*.

One afternoon the air was like cotton wool. I took Davey out in his stroller, around and around the *xiaochu*. Mimi and Ray Ray's grandfather advised me it was too cold to be out walking, though it wasn't particularly cold. It was a grey and misty afternoon, Irish and dreamy. There weren't the usual crowds around and the people who passed looked at us with concern. There was a heavy smell of industry. When I took Davey back up to the apartment, there were wads of black snot in his tiny nostrils.

A few days later everyone was talking about the severity of the air pollution. Lin and I got apps for our phones that told us the current PM 2.5 rating. It was like a weather app, and there were different backgrounds for different levels of pollution. Usually the screen was black as the pollution hung about up above the limitation of the rating scale, at 800 or so. The airpocalypse we called it.

We got two big air-cleaners into the apartment, and ran them constantly. They sounded like jet engines. We thought about putting duct tape around the seals of the windows, and maybe the door at night, but we never did this. Foreign teachers came to tell me they were having asthma attacks. There were a few midnight getaways. We put air cleaners into HQ and the centres, and created free-breathing zones.

The construction of my new apartment at Rong Jingcheng was completed and I received the key. This was the first home I had ever owned. We visited and I carried Davey on my shoulders around the landscaped paths and ponds. He ran on stiff legs across a Chinese bridge over to a pagoda on a little island, where we had a photo taken.

Lin Zhe hired a guy and we visited entire districts full of building materials. We spent weeks searching for lights, tiles, bathrooms and kitchens. We did a great job of decorating the 90 square metre apartment with ornate wood, alabaster, and sombre Italian marble. Perhaps interior decoration was my ultimate talent, and this 90 square metres will prove to have been the highest expression of my soul.

After the renovations were complete we left the apartment empty for six months to allow the poisons to settle. I set up an easel and a two by half metre canvas in the unfurnished apartment. I would get away from Aihua and spend the afternoons alone here, painting, smoking hash and listening to Boards of Canada, *Tomorrow's Harvest*.

I painted a story for Davey with Icarus, St Brendan, Tang San Zhang and his disciples, and a golden dragon pouring down over clouds in the centre as the source of light. Icarus was to the far left, with Deadalus off in the distance. Tan Shang Zhang and his disciples were climbing the clouds in the centre. I told Davey his *gan ma* was Tan Sang Zhang. St Brendan was to the right, alone in a curragh with shadowy sea-beasts around him. I was trying to portray the three stages of life.

The painting wasn't very good. When I showed it to Mike and Rob, I could tell they didn't like it, and were perhaps even a little embarrassed to be shown it. There was so much distance between what I saw, and what I was able to put on canvas. Perhaps if I'd had 10,000 years to develop technical skill I could have made this painting beautiful, I could have let my rage and sadness sing by bending the strings of a guitar, could have learned Chinese and written short, quiet Chinese poems, could have made this memoir something better than it is, something that would adequately communicate my vision. Still, the plain blue of the sky that covers most of the canvas is pleasant to look at.

After I finished this painting, Dan's son, Aaron, arrived to stay with us for a while. He had been a champion wrestler, and then when driving a pick up truck through Saskatchewan he'd been hit by a drunk guy driving on the wrong side of the highway. He lost his left arm and his left leg was twisted around backwards. He told me about this, about hanging upside down with the seat belt still on, while we stood at the window by the elevator in Rayda smoking, and drinking beer. It had been less than two years since the accident, and he was having trouble coping.

I got another two by half metre canvas and put it on the easel in my office in Wanshan. I had been thinking about a pair of Daedalian wings for Davey. I wanted to give him things that he could remember, artefacts which would last, that he could look at when he was old and think my daddy made these for me when I was little, and I remember.

I remembered my grandfather had told me about Daedalus and Icarus that one time I met him, that week that floats like a strange island. I wanted Davey to have a memory like this. My father told me that grandfather Cotter was the first man in Donegal to read *Ulysses*. I thought about putting the slogan *to fall and fly again* beneath the wings but I never got around to that.

Aaron and I painted the wings in the office, and then he would disappear somewhere in Beijing. I took him to train with the Shaolin guys, who were now at a university compound down in Feng Tai. We drove to Mentougou, and he stood on a barren peak and raised his arm over his head, quoting Icarus with one arm. I took a photo with my phone. It was sad but also brilliant.

We didn't finish painting the wings before he returned to Canada. I set up a camera on a tripod in my office, and filmed pairs of foreign teachers and Chinese staff finishing it off. While I explained to Julie how to paint the white on smoothly along the length of the feathers, I noticed Cindy painting vigorously up and down, going over the black outlines Aaron and I had painted so carefully.

After we completed the wings, Dylan Storz helped me paint a bloody, two-valved heart in the centre, between the wings. Over the following mornings I painted the arteries from the heart becoming twigs and leaves behind the wings before all hell would break loose at about 10:00 am.

I put together a video about the painting of the wings, and about Aihua's pedagogy, and put it on the Aihua website. I used the piano introduction from *Misty*, by Kate Bush, for the sound track. I was in China, so I never had to worry about copyright. The voice-over on this film told about my first memory of my grandfather, him lifting a leaf with two fingers to show me strawberries beneath.

It's strange, there are two early memories that have always been floating around my mind, coming to the surface now and then, but they were disparate, two fragments. I have only recognised their sequence since I have been working on this thing.

I was taken to stay with my grandparents in Omagh after the boy across the road from us in Belfast smashed a broom down with a Big Bang on my forehead. I remember so clearly the broom coming down from way up.

That was it. My awakening. How could I have been anything other than what I was. I was three years old. It was 1969.

I remember crying with blood in my eyes and all over my hands and the doorknob at our house in Belfast while my mother screamed at my father, but what could he do? He was a gentle man, and anyway, what sort of a name is Cotter, and then they took me to stay at my grandparents' house for a week or so, or maybe until we left for Canada. My grandmother stopped at a barricade and my aunt Rosemary, a young nurse in white, skipped between the sandbags into the hospital, between soldiers looking out from under helmets. There was a bombed building and when my grandfather told me it was bombed in the war, I thought he meant the one with Stukas, like Peter's model, that he had been so angry about when I broke the antennae.

This bang on the head, and this week with my grandparents, is the first thing that I remember, the sequence at the very start of it all, my waking up from nothingness. These memories float in blackness like a small archipelago before the continents of my memory proper begin.

For weeks through Chinese New Year the fireworks went off like armageddon outside our window. The pollution was up around eight and nine hundred, and I underwent my second lockdown. Schools were closed and people were told to stay indoors. We kept the air cleaners running around the clock. We got masks with valves at the side but Davey wouldn't wear his, even when I told him he looked like a spaceman.

During this lockdown, I organised Wechat activities for our students to keep the foreign teachers busy, and keep Aihua in the parents' eyes. I placed Fredrik in charge of timetabling the apartment-bound foreign teachers, and I read out the daily nursery rhyme first thing every morning. I soon ran out of nursery rhymes and had to use animal poems by Ted Hughes. For the rest of the day we heaped praise on the kids as they repeated back the nursery rhymes. There was a constant buzz of notifications. We had to ask the parents not to send messages after 8 pm.

An American guy I knew from James Joyce conferences in another life, Richard Stack, wrote to ask me if I'd be interested in writing a review of a book on China written by a friend of his. I downloaded the book from a torrent and went through it. I had no intention of writing a review of this book, but I read it through as though I would. The book was about China's persecution of dissidents, and it had stories of torture and disappearances. This was not the China I knew. The people I knew loved and respected China and its government. I realised though that the claims made by this book were also true.

There were foreign teachers at the school who were into Chomsky. Governments are all evil webs of brutal totalitarian lies. It is the nature of the beast. I wouldn't defend the Chinese government, but neither would I defend the Americans. If I say that Chinese people are like this or that, I am in error. If I say that this government is like this or that, I am also talking through my hat. There is never a whole truth. I can't comment on people or the government, but I can comment on what I've seen, and that is in many ways a culture that seemed kinder and wiser than the one I grew up in.

We sent Davey to a nursery at another apartment in Rongjingchang. One afternoon when I went down with Lin to collect Davey from the nursery school, I noticed Davey didn't seem himself. He stood there in his big jacket with a worried little face, not moving. The weight of the world seemed to be on his shoulders.

Lin stayed down with the other parents and kids and I went up to prepare dinner. I was drinking beer out by the elevators when she called me in a panic and told me to come down, something had happened to Davey's arm.

Her face was white when I got down. Davey stood beside her like a little ghost. Some of the grandparents had told her that something was wrong with Davey's arm. As we got Davey into the car, he began to cry with pain. Every movement brought tears and groans. I drove like Batman to the 301 hospital just as it was getting dark. We got him to a doctor, and he took one look at Davey then pushed the little arm back into its socket. I thanked him with tears in my eyes.

I managed to get from Davey that a teacher at the nursery had pulled him when he wouldn't go with her. We told the other parents what had happened but apart from some very dirty looks, and rantings about heads on poles, there was not much else I could do.

When Davey was four we sent him to kindergarten. Chen Fu used some *guanxi* and we paid a bribe to get him into Jing Yuan Kindergarten, which was attached to Jing Yuan Primary School, across the road at the back gates of our community. It was very convenient to take Davey there, but he hated it.

Jing Yuan was the most prestigious school in Shijingshan but I realised it could never suit Davey. At collection time, the parents gathered in a seething mob demanding their children. Two security guards stood at the narrow gate, in stab-vests and helmets. One held a pole with a u-shape fixed to one end, for catching people up against a wall, and the other cradled an electric baton. Davey looked stunned as he stepped between the guards, and took my hand amidst the surging mob. We eventually took him to a private kindergarten off Huafeilu, where the headmistress was raking in the dough, and uninterested in cooperating with Aihua. It was five kilometres away, and this was usually an hour raging at traffic.

When doing tests for her relentless hay fever, Chen Xi was diagnosed with lung cancer. She stopped coming into Aihua, and told me that she was trying to find a surgeon with a good reputation, to whom she could pay a bribe. She said that otherwise she would be sliced up like a pig on a table, and used the edge of her hand to show me how this would work.

While she was away from Aihua, everything fell on my shoulders. I spent my days in emergency meetings with various members of the Chinese management team. Priscilla, my assistant, sat beside me, taking notes and offering translation. Aihua had become so big, and it felt like the whole show was unravelling. Ray, Ivy and Marco were gone, and Chen Fu wasn't coming in.

There were requests for money from different directions. The staff were accusing one another of being disloyal to Aihua, and coming to me for adjudication. It was common knowledge that some of our marketing guys were stealing from the school. One of them even boasted about having been able to buy a car with this money. The manager at our new Gu Cheng site kept quitting and coming back, and we had no recourse but to keep him on because he had the support of the Chinese teachers at the centre. I felt as if I was being encircled by sharks.

Cindy was having an affair with Chen Xi's assistant. In my office one day she was boasting about China's 10,000 years of culture. I told her that I had always heard it was 5,000 years. The debate became heated, and Cindy demanded that I should fire her. She stood in the main office shouting out to the other Chinese staff, am I the only one who will stand up to this *laowai*? He disrespects China and you are all afraid to do anything. She asked were there no men to stand up for China? Was it up to a woman to defend China's honour alone? Julie and Li Miao tried to calm her down until she stormed out of the office. She stopped at the door and said you have no talent, that's why you come to China.

Cindy had been working with Aihua for eight years and, according to labour law, if we fired her we had to pay her 100,000 RMB. My position was that she had quit, and not been fired.

While I was waiting at the hospital with Chen Xi's mom, Chen Fu, Chen Wei, Yang Yang, Tan and a handful of relatives for Chen Xi's surgery, Cindy sent me a message written in formal Chinese. It said that because Chinese was the legal language of China, all of our future communication needed to be in Chinese. She said that if I would not agree that I had fired her within the hour, she would report me to the the Women's Council for sexual harassment. When I showed the message to Chen Fu, he grunted wearily and passed the phone back to me.

We waited in the hall as they brought Chen Xi out on a gurney. She lifted her head and said in English wee, I'm going on a journey, before they wheeled her between us toward the operating theatre.

When it was done, and they wheeled her back down the hall to her room, she was conscious, but inarticulate with pain, a small, groaning form beneath blankets. I kept asking why is she not sleeping? When we got to the room I was shaking.

Tan took charge, and had all the men gather round to slide her from the gurney to the bed. As we lifted her I saw tubes connected to her body, and she cried out in pain. I stood against the wall sobbing.

Cindy sent an email to all past and present Aihua staff, accusing me of many things. Lin translated key points from the email she had received as we sat beside Davey's blue buggy in the garden at Rong Jingcheng. Cindy called me a big cannon, which was a reference to the British guns used to destroy the Summer Palace in 1860. She reported me to the Women's Council, and Li Miao and Julie talked me through the accusations in my office, with the aid of Priscilla's translation.

Cindy said that I'd placed my head on her breast here in this office. This is something that I would never have done. I pointed out that the door to my office was glass, and that anyone could look in at any time. Julie and Li Miao went to the Women's Council and cleared up the matter. Cindy continued to have lunches with key members of our Aihua staff, including Julie and Li Miao. Eventually Chen Fu and Tan agreed to pay her off.

Chen Xi stayed in the hospital for a while, and she suffered a lot of pain. When I visited her, Tan would leave the room, and she told me I shouldn't stay long. Tan was devoted to looking after her.

When Chen XI got out of hospital, she didn't come back to the school, and I would meet with her and Tan in their apartment. We agreed to try and sell the school, and Tan began to look for a buyer.

While Chen Xi was away, we moved our headquarters from Wanshan to our final location in Yuangzhang. We were in an area designated for private education, among a handful of bizarre, old-fashioned kindergartens. The building was entered through a raised, walled compound full of rusted iron jungle-gyms, seesaws, and simple exercise machines for old people. Beside the door into our offices and classrooms was a two story billboard of me, standing in a suit, touching the knot of my purple tie.

This was my grandest representation yet, in the corner of a little shithole where no one could see it anyway, except for the brief instant they turned the corner to come into the building. I think this billboard may have been somebody's idea of a joke, maybe Fan Cheng's–regardless, there it was every morning: the smug, self satisfied grin, the face I detested, Buck Mulligan.

We were well away from the subway and from any straight roads in an unremarkable community north of Gucheng. The location was convenient however to Gu Er primary school, and we sent Chinese and foreign teachers together to collect the students from the school gates, and walk them through the hectic hutons to our shoddy new school. We shed a lot of management staff, mostly marketing people.

Chen Xi and I shared an office, but she rarely came in, and when she did she only stayed a few minutes before we slipped off for sushi at Sam's Club, or to a *jiaoziguar* near her apartment. She would tell me about Tan's progress in finding a buyer, and we would fantasise about being free of Aihua.

When Xi Jing Ping began his crusade against Tigers and Flies, stamping down on corruption, there was no one that we could turn to when we had trouble. A dinner and an affectionate bribe could no longer solve problems. The police dropped into our Zhongguancun centre and took the foreign teachers to the station.

They were released in the evening, and instructed to return to the station the next morning. I went with them, and brought Priscilla, Julie and Li Miao. The officers were young and officious. There was no older guy you could have a *biajiou* with and flatter a bit. They didn't even seem to smoke.

The problem was that our licensing for foreign teachers was only valid for Shijingshan, but Zhongguancun was in Haidian. The officers made clear that I was not a legal representative of the company, and that they had no business with me, a mere foreign teacher. They insisted that they needed to see Chen Xi. I tried to tell them Chen Xi was just out of hospital, but their attitude was vindictive. At first they let on that they couldn't understand my Chinese, and then told me in English that nothing I said was relevant.

Chen Xi spent the next two days running in and out of the Foreign Affairs police station in Haidian. She seemed weak, and I wanted to protect her, but there was no alternative. She managed to solve the problem, and we were able to return to teaching at Zhongguancun.

Tan was looking after Chen Xi very well, cooking for her, coddling her, and she was starting to recover. She and I continued to meet for sushi or dumplings at lunch. I was handing more and more of my responsibilities over to Fred, Rob Warman, and the seven Center Senior Foreign Teachers. I was never in any hurry to get back from lunch with Chen Xi to HQ at Yuangzhang.

When Tan found an interested buyer, Chen Xi and I began to fantasise about what we would do after we had the money, and were away. I told Chen Xi I wanted to build a *siheyuar* in a forest in Norway, with a wall of the courtyard for her and Tan. We talked about Thailand. She told me that we should be very grateful to Tan for finding us a buyer, and I agreed.

I was getting ready to go into the Christmas brunch at Pullman's with the foreign teachers when Chen Xi called me and told me we had received the down payment from the buyers, and that she had already transferred half of this money to my account.

I went into Pullman's with Lin and Davey. All the foreign teachers were there. There were two turkeys, two hams and all the trimmings. There were Christmas trees and they were playing Christmas music. The foreign teachers had been having Christmas brunch at Pullman's for about three years. As soon as I got in, at 10:30 am, I started drinking whiskey. There was champagne and mulled wine, which I also needed to try. After lunch, when we moved to the bar, I was plastered. Lin took Davey home.

I was talking utter shite. I called one teacher aside and whispered to him that I had just bought a forest in Sweden. He said congratulations on the plot of land, and I said, no, no, you don't understand, it's a forest. I started arguing with Karl O'Dwyer, who was such a nice young GAA lad from Trim, and the next thing we were wrestling from the bar into the foyer. He was stronger than me, and he got me down, which I couldn't bear, so I rallied and was standing above him with my hands pressing his face into the marble.

I was angry because I knew I was getting slower and weaker. The signals weren't moving as quickly from my brain. I let out a string of profanities before letting his head go. I continued to curse him with filthy language, and the Turkish manager tried to calm me down, telling me there were police in the hotel. I didn't care about the police, I told them. I moved around talking to the foreign teachers, getting drunker and drunker. Nolan Kinney told me I was that uncle.

I was delivered home in a cab by Rob Warman. He wouldn't stay, and he told us I had been saying terrible things about him in the cab. I didn't remember, and I didn't believe him.

I awoke with a start beside Lin the next morning. Large hunks of my memory had been torn away, and I couldn't reassemble the events of the day before. I started making calls, to find out if anything worse than what I remembered had happened.

Trish Flahive, the Gucheng Senior Foreign Teacher, didn't answer my call. When I got through to Fred, he refused to paint a rosy picture. Rob was not willing to say much. I noticed that Trish Flahive and Aoife O'Donnell had dropped me as friends on facebook.

Fred phoned Chen Xi the day after and told her about my behaviour at the Christmas party. He asked her not to tell me he'd told her. When she told me, she said don't worry, we're getting away from this shit.

I couldn't only blame this on the drink. Why did I drink like this in the first place? Why did I keep doing this again and again, even now, when I had Davey? Could I never escape myself, say enough, it's done. Thick black snakes coiled where my brain should have been, their torpid lives feeding on the tender marrow of my life. It is so easy to say look, there goes a man with no talent.

We signed a contract to provide teacher training to all of the public school English teachers in Shijingshan. It was to be all day, five days a week, for a month. The Education Committee insisted that I should be the teacher, but I got them to agree to have a group of foreign teachers for the first two periods of each day, and these teachers broke them into groups of five.

When I arrived I taught all 40 teachers as one group for the rest of the day. This was the kind of teaching that I was good at, and these were the kinds of students I was good at teaching: disillusioned, modest, realistic. We got on well. We talked about life. Between classes I would pace back and forth in a corner outside with my arms locked behind my back, resisting the urge to smoke.

Beijing was snowy and polluted. It felt like the end of the world. I listened to *Hinterland*, by Recondite, while walking along the decommissioned steel mill from our apartment in Rongjingchen to the Shijingshan Education Bureau in Gucheng. Near an old railway line that used to run into Shougang, I saw red chillies cascading from the back of a truck, and in the grime and cotton wool air, all of the meaning in the world was pulled into this red.

Fred was managing the school while I was doing the teacher training. He needed to know how to do this because he was part of our deal with the buyer.

I met with Chen Xi in Gucheng Park at lunchtime each day between my classes, and we strolled round the pagodas, arching bridges and shallow pools. The white haze of the pollution, and the shady corners of grimy snow, imbued the park with an otherworldly quality. It became the ghost of an ancient Chinese city. There were delays and legal complications in closing the deal with the buyers, and we could not bear to hope anymore, as our dreams sagged round us, and the last of the colour sept away.

When the money came through, the handover of Aihua was swift. Chen Xi paid tax and then transferred my share to me. We agreed on something for Chen Fu, and for Swan. We handed over our desks at Yuangzhang to Mr Fan and Mr Liu, and then Chen Fu, Tan, Chen Xi and I sat in a little Xinjiang place nearby, drinking beer, laughing like pirates with the *err* of the *Beijinghua*, smiling widely to tug hunks of spicy lamb from the sticks with our teeth. I was not eager to say goodbye.